From *Frankenstein*

After many days and nights of intense labor and fatigue, Victor discovered how to create life from lifeless matter. He felt astonishment, then joy.

Victor wondered whether he should attempt to create a human or a simpler creature. He decided to create a human. Because it would be easier to make large, crude muscles and veins than to fashion more-intricate parts, he decided to make a gigantic human, about eight feet tall.

From *The Strange Case of Dr. Jekyll and Mr. Hyde*

He put the glass to his lips and drank the mixture in one gulp. A cry followed. He reeled, staggered, clutched at the table, and held on. Staring and gasping, he swelled. His face turned black, and his features melted.

I sprang to my feet and leaped back against the wall. My arms were raised to shield me from what I saw. I was overcome with terror. "Oh, God!" I screamed again and again.

FRANKENSTEIN and
THE STRANGE CASE OF
DR. JEKYLL AND MR. HYDE

TP THE TOWNSEND LIBRARY

For more titles in the Townsend Library,
visit our website: **www.townsendpress.com**

All new material in this edition is
copyright © 2005 by Townsend Press.
Printed in the United States of America

09876

Illustrations © 2005 by Hal Taylor

Townsend Press, Inc.
439 Kelley Drive
West Berlin, New Jersey 08091

ISBN-13: 978-1-59194-052-4
ISBN-10: 1-59194-052-4

Library of Congress Control Number:
2005925623

FRANKENSTEIN

The Strange Case of DR. JEKYLL AND MR. HYDE

 THE TOWNSEND LIBRARY

A Background Note about *Frankenstein*

As early as 1838, twenty years after *Frankenstein*'s publication, someone referred to mules as "Frankensteins" because a mule is the offspring of a donkey and a horse. Frankenstein's title character is experimenter Victor Frankenstein, not the creature he creates. Nevertheless, the word Frankenstein very quickly came to mean a monster, especially one with the power to wreak destruction.

FRANKENSTEIN

MARY WOLLSTONECRAFT SHELLEY

Edited, and with an Afterword,
by Joan Dunayer

Alphonse Frankenstein was a wealthy, distinguished man of Geneva, Switzerland. He was a highly respected member of the Swiss government known for his integrity and tireless devotion to public service. Because he was so single-minded in this devotion, he married late in life. His wife, Caroline, was much younger than he, but they dearly loved each other. Alphonse revered Caroline for her goodness and loved to please and protect her. In 1772, they had their first child, Victor.

Victor was an extremely happy child who adored his doting parents. When he was five, his parents adopted a four-year-old orphan named Elizabeth. A slender, beautiful child, she had fair skin, golden hair, bright blue eyes, a high forehead, and perfectly formed features. Her voice was soft and melodious. Her gentle smile shed radiance.

From the beginning, Victor loved Elizabeth. In all his occupations and pleasures, Elizabeth was his adored companion. Victor and Elizabeth were in perfect harmony. Whereas she was calm, sweet, and artistic—a lover of poetry and natural beauty—he was passionate, quick-tempered, and eager to obtain scientific knowledge.

Victor was a private person, indifferent to most of his schoolmates, but he formed a close friendship with one of them, Henry Clerval, the son of a businessman. Henry had singular talent and imagination. He loved adventure, danger, and books of chivalry and romance. He wrote songs and tales about enchantment and knightly adventure. He led Victor and other boys in acting out plays about knights. Thoughtful, kind, generous, and high-spirited, Henry wanted to be a hero and great benefactor of humankind. Whereas Victor was interested in science, Henry loved languages and literature.

In 1787, when Victor was fifteen, his brother William was born. That same year, his mother caught scarlet fever from a poor family whom she had assisted out of charity. As she lay dying, she put Victor's hand into Elizabeth's and said, "My children, I've always hoped that you would marry. Such a union would greatly console your father. Elizabeth, my love, be a mother to William. I hate to leave all of you. I've been so

happy and loved. But I expect to see all of you again in Heaven." She died calmly, with her face expressing love.

Three years later, Victor prepared to depart for the University of Ingolstadt, in Germany. The evening before Victor's departure, Henry came to the Frankensteins' house to say good-bye. He wished that he, too, could attend a university. But his narrow-minded father wouldn't permit it. Victor and Henry sat up late, finding it hard to part company. At last, they went to bed.

At dawn, when Victor went down to the carriage, his father, Henry, and Elizabeth were there waiting for him. His father blessed him, Henry pressed his hand, and Elizabeth begged him to write often. In misery, Victor entered the carriage, which set off for Ingolstadt.

Having always been surrounded by loving companions, Victor suddenly was alone, soon to be among strangers. Only one thought lifted his spirits: he would be acquiring new knowledge.

The journey was long and tiring. Finally Victor saw the high, white steeple of Ingolstadt's church.

Victor spent his first few days at Ingolstadt becoming acquainted with the town and the residents in his dormitory, in which he had an apartment of several rooms.

The first lecture he attended was given by

Franz Waldman, a professor of physiology. Waldman was about fifty. He had a kind face. His hair was gray at his temples but otherwise black. He was short but straight-postured. Waldman began his lecture with a brief history of physiology, enthusiastically recounting great discoveries. He then explained many of physiology's basic terms and gave an overview of modern physiology. "Great physiologists peer into nature's hiding places and uncover its secrets," he said. "They have discovered how we breathe and how the blood circulates."

"So much has been done," Victor thought, "but I'll do more. I'll discover great things."

The next day, Victor went to see Waldman at his home. The professor welcomed him warmly. Victor said how much he had appreciated Waldman's lecture and asked the professor to recommend books that he should read.

"I'm happy to have a student such as you," Waldman said. "If you're as hardworking as you are capable, I have no doubt that you'll succeed. If your wish is to become a genuine scientist, not merely a petty experimenter, I advise you to study mathematics and every branch of science."

Waldman took Victor into his laboratory and explained the uses of his various scientific instruments. He also gave Victor the book list that he had requested.

From that day on, science—especially physiology—was Victor's obsession. He eagerly read science books, attended all the science lectures that he could, cultivated the acquaintance of the university's scientists, and sometimes studied and experimented until dawn.

Waldman became a true friend. He was a frank, good-natured person and an excellent teacher.

Victor made rapid progress, astonishing both his teachers and his fellow students. He even made some discoveries regarding ways to improve scientific instruments. He became increasingly interested in the causes of life.

Victor had no religious beliefs. He thought that everything had a scientific explanation. To him, a graveyard was nothing more than a place where lifeless bodies are buried. He felt that to learn the causes of life, he must study death. So he examined the causes of decay, spending days and nights in burial vaults and charnel houses. He saw how a person's eyes and brain became food for worms.

After many days and nights of intense labor and fatigue, Victor discovered how to create life from lifeless matter. He felt astonishment, then joy.

Victor wondered whether he should attempt to create a human or a simpler creature.

He decided to create a human. Because it would be easier to make large, crude muscles and veins than to fashion more-intricate parts, he decided to make a gigantic human, about eight feet tall.

For months, Victor gathered the necessary materials. He took body parts from slaughtered animals and human corpses.

He was thrilled. "A new race of humans will bless me as its creator," he thought. "Many happy, excellent beings will owe their existence to me. No father deserves his child's gratitude more than I'll deserve theirs. Perhaps, with time, I'll also be able to bring the dead back to life."

Pale and thin from too much work, he eagerly began assembling all the parts. His laboratory was in a solitary, top-floor room separated from all the other apartments by a hallway and staircase.

The summer passed. Victor paid no attention to nature's beauty and nearly forgot his absent loved ones. His father wrote, expressing concern at Victor's not having written in quite some time. But Victor couldn't tear himself from his experiment.

Another year passed the same way. Every night, Victor was feverish. He became extremely nervous. The fall of a leaf was enough to startle him. He shunned other people as if he were guilty of a crime. Sometimes his condition alarmed him, but he was determined to finish his creation.

On a dreary November night, Victor beheld the results of his efforts. With sharp anxiety, he prepared to infuse the spark of life into the life-less thing that lay on the table before him. It was 1 a.m. Rain pattered dismally against the window-panes. His candle was nearly burned out.

Then, by the glimmer of the half-extin-guished light, Victor saw the creature's dull yellow eyes open. The creature breathed hard. A convulsive motion agitated his limbs.

Victor had taken great pains to make the creature beautiful. The creature's hair was shiny black and flowing. His teeth were pearly white. However, by contrast, these features made his other features look more ghastly. The creature's skin was yellow and shriveled and scarcely covered the muscles and veins beneath. His eyes were watery and nearly the same brownish gray as their sockets. His lips were straight and black.

For nearly two years, Victor had worked with the goal of infusing life into an inanimate body. He had deprived himself of rest and health. Now he felt horror and disgust. Unable to endure the appearance of the being he had created, he hurried from the room and paced in his bedroom. Finally, exhaustion overcame him. Still dressed, he threw himself onto his bed and slept.

Victor had nightmares. He thought he saw Elizabeth, in the bloom of health, walking in Ingolstadt. Delighted and surprised, he embraced her. But as he kissed her lips, they took on a deathlike color. Her features changed, and Victor held his mother's corpse. It was draped in flannel; worms crawled in the folds.

Victor started from his sleep. A cold sweat covered his forehead. His teeth chattered. His limbs convulsed. The moon's dim, yellow light forced its way through the window shutters, and he beheld the creature he had created.

The creature held up the bed curtain. His eyes were fixed on Victor. His jaws opened, and he muttered some inarticulate sounds. A grin wrinkled his cheeks. He stretched out a hand, to touch Victor, but Victor fled downstairs.

Victor took refuge in the courtyard, where he remained the rest of the night, pacing, listening intently, fearing that every sound announced the creature's approach. "A mummy come to life couldn't be as hideous as that monster," he thought.

Victor passed the night wretchedly. Sometimes his heart beat so quickly and violently that he seemed to feel every artery pulsing. Sometimes he nearly sank to the ground from weakness and exhaustion. Along with horror, he felt bitter disappointment. His dream had become a nightmare.

Dismal and wet, morning finally dawned. Victor's sleepless, aching eyes saw the clock in the church tower: 6 a.m. Victor went into the street, walking quickly. Every time he turned a street corner, he feared that he would see the creature. He didn't dare return to his apartment. He hurried on, drenched by the rain that poured from a black, comfortless sky.

Victor continued walking for some time, trying to ease his distress through exercise. He walked without any clear idea as to where he was or what he was doing. His heart pounded in fear.

Finally, he came to the inn at which coaches commonly stopped. He paused and watched a coach that was coming toward him. The coach stopped just where he was standing. When the door opened, he saw Henry Clerval.

Henry sprang out. "Victor!" he exclaimed. "I'm so glad to see you! How fortunate that you should be here at the very moment of my arrival!"

Victor was overjoyed to see Henry, whose presence brought back thoughts of Victor's father, Elizabeth, William, and all the scenes of home so dear to Victor's memory. Victor grasped Henry's hand and forgot his horror and misfortune. For the first time in many months, he felt peace and joy. He warmly welcomed his friend, and the two walked toward Victor's dormitory.

"It gives me the greatest delight to see you," Victor said. "How are my father, William, and Elizabeth?"

"Well and happy, only a little worried that they hear from you so seldom." Henry stopped short and gazed at Victor's face. "You look ill and exhausted. You're pale and thin."

"Lately I've been so involved in a project that I haven't allowed myself much rest. I hope to return to other things now." Victor trembled, thinking of the previous night.

"I feel so lucky to be here," Henry said. "You can easily guess how hard it was for me to persuade my father that bookkeeping isn't the sum of all necessary knowledge. Finally, his affection for me overcame his distrust of intellectual pursuits, and he permitted me to journey to the land of knowledge."

As the two friends walked, Henry talked about mutual friends.

Victor, however, scarcely listened. With a shiver, he wondered if the creature was still in his apartment, alive and walking around. He dreaded to behold him, but he feared even more that Henry might see him.

Upon arriving at the dormitory, Victor asked Henry to remain at the bottom of the stairs for a few minutes. Victor darted up to his room. Fearing what he would see, he threw open the door. Nothing unusual. Fearfully, he stepped in. With joy, he concluded that the creature must have fled.

Henry joined Victor in the apartment, and a servant brought them breakfast. Victor was so relieved that he was giddy. He jumped around, clapped his hands, and laughed loudly.

The wildness in his eyes, and his loud, unrestrained laughter alarmed Henry. "Victor," he said, "for God's sake, what's the matter with you? Why are you laughing like that? Are you ill?"

Victor's terror of the creature returned, and he fainted. For several months, he was bedridden with a nervous fever. Henry was his only nurse. Victor kept picturing the creature. He constantly raved concerning him. At first, Henry thought that Victor was delirious, but he soon became convinced that Victor's illness was the result of some strange and terrible event.

Slowly Victor got well. A beautiful spring greatly contributed to his recovery. Buds shot forth from the trees that shaded his window. His gloom disappeared. He became as cheerful as he had been before becoming obsessed with his experiment.

"Henry," he said. "You've been so good to me. This whole winter, instead of studying as you had intended, you've been my nurse. How can I ever repay you? I'm so sorry for the disappointment that I've caused. Forgive me."

"You'll entirely repay me if you don't upset yourself. Get well as fast as you can. Since you appear to be in such good spirits, I'd like to speak to you about something."

Victor trembled. Was it possible that Henry knew about the creature?

Seeing Victor pale, Henry said, "Calm yourself, Victor. I just wanted to say that your father and Elizabeth would be very happy if they received a letter from you. They've been worried by your long silence."

"Is that all, Henry? Of course I'll write to them."

"Good. Here's a letter from Elizabeth."

In her letter, Elizabeth told Victor all the news from home. "You should see William," she wrote. "He's so sweet and loving. And he's a beautiful child, tall for his age. He has merry blue eyes, dark eyelashes, and curling hair. When he smiles, two dimples appear on each cheek, which are rosy with health." Elizabeth's letter concluded, "Your father and I have been worried that you're ill. He has wanted to travel to see you, but I've persuaded him not to, because he isn't strong anymore. Please let us hear from you."

"Dear Elizabeth!" Victor said. "I'll write immediately and relieve them of anxiety."

Two weeks later, Victor was well enough to leave his rooms. He introduced Henry to several professors. However, ever since the creature had come to life, Victor had felt a hatred of science. The mere sight of a physiology lab caused him extreme distress.

Henry had come to the university to study Asian languages, especially Persian, Arabic, and Sanskrit. Inspired by his friend's enthusiasm, Victor, too, turned to language studies.

About a year later, Victor received a letter from his father informing him that William had been murdered—strangled. Victor hurried home to Geneva. He wept to see the mountains, streams, and beautiful lake of his home region.

It was completely dark when he arrived in Geneva. The city's gates already were shut for the night, so he went to a nearby village for lodging. Unable to sleep, he headed back out, to the place where William had been murdered. Previously clear, the sky now clouded over. A storm approached. The rain started falling slowly, in large drops. Its violence quickly increased.

Victor walked on, although the darkness and storm increased every minute and the thunder crashed over his head. The mountains echoed the thunder. Vivid flashes of lightning dazzled Victor's eyes, illuminating Lake Geneva, making it look like a vast sheet of fire. Then, for an instant, everything went dark, until Victor's eyes recovered from the previous flash.

While Victor watched the storm, beautiful but frightening, he wandered on with a hasty step. "William!" he exclaimed in grief when he reached the place where the murder had occurred.

In the gloom a figure emerged from behind a nearby clump of trees.

Victor stood fixed with fear and horror, staring. A flash of lightning illuminated the figure and plainly revealed its deformity and gigantic stature. Victor immediately recognized the creature. "Filthy demon!" he thought. "What is he doing here?" Then, with a shudder, he thought, "He must be William's murderer!" Victor leaned against a tree for support.

The figure quickly passed and disappeared into the gloom. Victor thought of pursuing him, but it was futile. Another flash revealed the creature hanging from the rocks of a steep mountainside. He soon reached the summit and disappeared.

Victor remained motionless. The thunder ceased, but the rain continued. The scene was enveloped in darkness. Victor considered the events that he had tried to forget: his progress toward the act of creation, the creature's appearance at his bedside, and the creature's departure. More than a year had passed since the creature's birth. Was William's murder the creature's first crime? Victor thought, "Oh, my God! I've turned loose into the world a depraved wretch who delights in killing."

Victor spent the rest of the night in the open air. Cold and wet, he suffered, but not because of the weather. He imagined scenes of evil and despair. He considered the being whom he had cast among humankind and endowed with the will and power to commit horrible crimes, such as William's murder. "He's like a vampire version of myself," he thought, "like my own evil spirit let loose from the grave and driven to destroy all that I cherish."

Day dawned, and Victor walked toward Geneva. The city's gates were open, and he hurried to his father's house. At first he planned to reveal what he knew about the murderer and have him pursued. But he paused when he thought about the story that he would have to tell. A being whom he had formed and endowed with life had killed his brother. If he told anyone that, they would think him insane. Besides, the creature would elude capture, even if people could be persuaded to pursue him. The creature could scale the sides of the steepest mountain.

So Victor decided not to reveal anything.

When he entered his father's house, it was about 5 a.m. He told the servants not to disturb Elizabeth and his father. Years had passed since he had left for Ingolstadt. "Beloved and venerable father!" he thought. Victor gazed on the picture of his mother that hung over the mantelpiece. Below this picture was a miniature of William. When Victor saw it, he wept.

Victor's father soon entered. Unhappiness was deeply etched into his face, but he tried to welcome his son cheerfully.

Then Elizabeth came in. Time had altered her. She was even more beautiful than as a teenager. She had the same candor and vivacity, but her face now also showed exquisite sensitivity and intellect. She welcomed Victor with the greatest affection. "My dear friend, your arrival gives me hope."

Victor perceived Elizabeth's deep, voiceless grief. "I'm the cause of her suffering!" he thought. "And my father's. Before they were so happy. Now they're miserable. And William. . . . He's dead because of me. He's dead, and I'm alive."

Despair and remorse pressed on Victor's heart. For weeks, he slept only for brief spells. He had committed deeds of horror, yet his heart overflowed with kindness and a love of virtue.

He had started life with good intentions and had longed for the time that he would make himself useful to other people. Now all of his hopes were blasted. Instead of the serenity bestowed by a clear conscience, he felt almost unbearable grief and guilt.

His state of mind undermined his health, which had never entirely recovered from the first shock of the creature's birth. He shunned company. He felt no ability to share others' joy. To the contrary, their joy tortured him. Solitude was his only comfort—death-like solitude.

Alphonse painfully observed the change in his son's disposition and habits and sought to ease his son's grief. "Do you think, Victor, that I don't suffer, too?" he asked. "No one could love a child more than I loved William." Tears came into his eyes as he spoke. "But don't we have a duty to the survivors to avoid increasing their unhappiness by displaying excessive grief? You also have a duty to yourself. Excessive sorrow prevents improvement or enjoyment. It even prevents a person from being useful. It renders them unfit for society."

Victor thought, "I'd be able to hide my grief and console my friends if I didn't also feel remorse and terror." Victor's only response to his father was a look of despair.

The next day, Victor, Elizabeth, and

Alphonse went to the family's country house about four miles from Geneva, on the shore of Lake Geneva. This change was particularly agreeable to Victor. Often, after Elizabeth and his father retired for the night, Victor took a boat and spent many hours on the lake. Sometimes, with the sails set, he was carried by the wind. Sometimes, after rowing into the middle of the lake, he let the boat follow its own course and he gave way to misery. He often was tempted to plunge into the silent lake, so that the waters would close over him forever.

He was restrained by thoughts of Elizabeth and his father. He felt he couldn't desert them, leaving them unprotected against the malice of the creature whom he had let loose among them.

Victor lived in daily fear that the creature would commit some new crime. He hated the creature. He wanted to extinguish the life that he had bestowed. He wanted to see the creature again, so that he could avenge William's death.

The Frankenstein house remained in mourning. The horror of William's murder had damaged Alphonse's health.

Elizabeth no longer delighted in her ordinary occupations. She no longer was the happy person who, in her earlier youth, had wandered with Victor on the banks of Lake Geneva and talked, with joy, of their future prospects. She grieved. "William was murdered," she said to Victor, "and his killer has escaped. He walks around free, perhaps respected."

Victor listened to her words with agony. "I'm the true murderer," he thought.

Seeing Victor's anguish, Elizabeth took his hand. "My dearest friend, calm yourself. William's murder has greatly affected me, God knows, but I'm not as wretched as you. Sometimes you have a look of despair and desire for revenge that frightens me. Dear Victor, banish these dark passions. Remember those who love you and center all their hopes in you. Have we lost the power to make you happy? As long as we love one another, and live in this wonderful country of peace and beauty, we are blessed."

But even Elizabeth's love couldn't comfort Victor. Even as she spoke, he feared that the creature might harm her. Nothing could relieve Victor's pain and despair. He felt like a wounded deer who drags himself to some secluded place to die, looking at the arrow that has pierced him.

Finally, desperate to find some relief, Victor traveled alone to the mountains. One day the rain was pouring in torrents; thick mists hid the mountains' peaks. Still, he ventured out for a mountain hike. He ascended higher and higher. He paused in a rock recess and gazed on the wonderful scenery before him. A vast river of ice wound among the mountains, whose icy and glittering peaks shone in the sunlight above the clouds. For a moment, Victor forgot his sorrow.

Then he saw someone, at a distance, coming toward him with superhuman speed. The figure bounded over ice crevices that had caused Victor to walk with caution. The figure's stature exceeded that of a man. Victor felt faint with alarm. As the shape came closer, he saw the creature. Trembling with rage and horror, Victor stood his ground, determined to fight the creature to the death.

The creature approached. His face showed anger, bitterness, and suffering.

Victor found him almost too hideous for human eyes. "Devil!" he cried. "How dare you approach me? Don't you fear my vengeance? I only wish that ending your miserable existence could restore William to life!"

"I expected this," the creature said. "Humans hate those who are wretched, and I'm wretched beyond all other living beings. Even you—my creator—detest and spurn me. You're bound to me by ties that only death can dissolve. You want to kill me. How dare you trifle thus with life? You created me. Now you want to destroy me. Do your duty toward me, and I'll do mine toward you and the rest of humankind. If you'll meet my conditions, I'll leave you and all other humans in peace. But if you refuse, I'll kill your remaining loved ones."

"Monster! Fiend! Hell's tortures would be too mild a punishment for your crimes. You blame me for your creation. Come on, then. Let me end the life that I so carelessly bestowed." Victor jumped at the creature, determined to kill him.

The creature easily eluded him. "Be calm! Hear me out before you vent your hatred. Haven't I suffered enough? Although I suffer, my life is dear to me, and I'll defend it. Remember, I'm more powerful than you. I'm bigger and stronger. My joints are more supple. Still, I don't want to fight you. I'm your creation. I'll be docile and devoted if you'll fulfill your obligations to me. Frankenstein, don't be fair to everyone else but unfair to me. You owe me justice, even forgiveness and affection, because you're the one responsible for my existence. You abandoned me when I had done nothing wrong. I sought love and kindness and found none. Grant me some happiness, and I'll be virtuous."

"Go away! I won't listen to you. There can be no friendship between us. We're enemies. Either go away, or fight me to the death."

"Will no amount of begging move you? Will nothing make you treat me with some fairness and kindness? Believe me, Frankenstein, I was good. My soul glowed with love and compassion. But you left me to be alone, miserably alone. Other humans hate and fear me. You, especially, owe me better treatment. I've suffered keenly. I've been forced to take refuge in icy caves far from humans. The most intense cold is kinder to me than humans are. If most humans knew of my existence, they'd seek my death. Humans have shown me nothing but injustice and cruelty. Why don't you call *them* monsters and fiends? Listen to my tale. When you've heard it, either pity me or, once again, abandon me. But hear me out. The law allows humans to speak in their own defense before they're condemned. You accuse me of murder, yet you'd like to murder me, your own creature. What hypocrites you humans are!"

"I curse the day, abhorred devil, that you first saw light! You've made me completely wretched. Go away! Relieve me of the sight of your detested form."

The creature put his hand over Victor's eyes, saying, "Hear me out, then, without looking at me."

Victor flung the creature's hand away.

"Listen to me. I demand this of you," the

creature insisted. "Come out of the cold now. Come to my hut on the mountain and hear my story. It depends on you whether the rest of my life will be harmless or I'll become the scourge of humankind and the cause of your own speedy ruin."

Reluctantly, Victor followed the creature across the ice. He felt both curiosity and some compassion. For one thing, he wanted to know, with certainty, whether or not the creature had killed William. For the first time, he also felt some duties toward the being he had created. "Shouldn't I try to help him rather than simply condemn him?" he thought.

The creature and Victor ascended. The air was cold, and it rained again. They entered the creature's hut, and he lit a fire. Victor sat by the fire, and the creature began his story.

"It is with considerable difficulty that I remember my origin," the creature said. "All the events of that period are confused and indistinct. At first, my senses were all jumbled: a mixture of sights, sounds, feelings, and smells. I remember entering your apartment and covering myself with some clothes before leaving. After walking around, I sought relief from the heat by entering the forest near Ingolstadt, where I rested beside a brook. Hungry and thirsty, I ate some berries that I found hanging from trees or lying on the ground. I drank from the brook. Then I slept.

"When I awoke, it was night. I felt cold and afraid. With the moon lighting my way, I searched for more berries. Under one of the trees I found a huge cloak, with which I covered myself. Several days later, my senses were more distinct. I saw and heard more clearly. I delighted in the moon, the foliage, and the sounds of birds. Sometimes I tried to imitate their songs, but I couldn't. At other times, I tried to express myself through my voice, but the crude, inarticulate sounds that came out frightened me into silence again.

"One day, when I was cold, I came across a fire that must have been left by some wandering beggars. Its warmth delighted me. I thrust my hand into the live embers but quickly pulled it back with a cry of pain. 'How strange,' I thought, 'that the same cause should produce such opposite effects!' I examined the fire and found it to be composed of wood, so I quickly gathered wood. When night came, I spread my cloak on the ground and slept.

"Food became scarce. I often spent the whole day searching in vain for a few acorns to eat. So I decided to look for a place with more food. Wrapping myself in my cloak, I headed toward the setting sun. After three days of walking through the forest, I reached open fields, covered with snow, which chilled my feet.

"I longed for food and shelter. Finally I saw a small shepherd's hut on a hill. The door was open, so I entered. An old man sat near a fire, preparing his breakfast. When he saw me, he shrieked and ran from the hut. I devoured his breakfast of bread, cheese, and milk. Then I lay down on some straw and slept.

"I awoke at noon, took all the food I could find, and proceeded across the fields for several hours. At sunset I arrived at a village. I entered an attractive cottage. Immediately, children shrieked and one of the women fainted. The whole village was alerted. Some villagers fled. Others attacked me, hurting me by throwing stones and other objects.

"I escaped to the open country and fearfully took refuge in a bare hovel so low that I barely could sit upright in it. The floor was dirt but dry. The wind entered through many chinks, but I was protected from snow and rain. The hovel was attached to the back of a neat, pleasant cottage. However, after my recent experience, I didn't dare enter the cottage.

"At dawn I carpeted my small shelter with clean straw. The shelter's nearness to the cottage's chimney provided warmth. After I ate some bread for breakfast, I heard someone approaching. Looking through a chink, I saw a lovely young woman in a blue dress. She had blond, braided hair and was carrying a pail of milk. Then I saw a handsome young man take the pail from her. They entered the cottage together.

"I found a chink in my shelter that allowed me to look into the cottage. I saw a small but clean room with meager furniture. An old, silver-haired man sat in one corner, near a small fire. He took up an instrument and produced beautiful sounds. The young woman sat nearby, knitting. The scene was utterly peaceful. Soon after, the young man came in, carrying a load of wood. The three ate a meal together. Throughout the day, the young woman and young man worked hard. The relationship among the three was clearly loving. It caused me to feel deep emotion, a combination of joy and pain.

"When night came, I saw that the cottagers prolonged light by using candles. 'How wonderful!' I thought. The young man read aloud. At the time, though, I knew nothing of words or their meanings.

"That night, I lay on my straw but couldn't sleep. I was struck by the cottagers' gentle manner. I longed to join them, but I remembered too well the treatment that I had suffered from the barbarous villagers.

"Each day, the cottagers rose before dawn, the young woman arranged the cottage and prepared the food, and the young man left after breakfast. The young woman spent the day doing inside chores, and the young man spent it doing outside ones. I soon perceived that the old man was blind. The young man and woman always showed affection and respect for him, which the old man returned.

"Because I didn't want to take food from such good people, I survived on berries, nuts, and roots, which I gathered from neighboring woods.

"I soon realized that humans spoke in words, which had meanings. I was anxious to learn to speak. After listening for several months, I realized that objects had names: *fire*, *milk*, *bread*, *wood*. So did people. The young woman was Agatha, the young man was Felix, and the old man was Father. Other words were harder for me to understand: *good*, *dearest*, *happy*.

"Throughout the winter, I sympathized with the cottagers and learned from them. When they felt sad, so did I. When they felt happy, I did too. At first, their reading aloud puzzled me. Then I realized that written words had meanings, just like spoken ones. I wanted to be able to read as well as speak. I thought that if I learned human language, I might be able to speak to humans without them hating me for my deformity.

"I thought the cottagers were beautiful. In contrast, when I viewed my reflection in a pool, I started back in horror, unable to believe that I really was seeing myself. When I realized that I truly was that hideous, I felt bitter shame and grief.

"Winter changed to spring, and I marveled at the earth's transformation. The birds sang in more cheerful notes, and flower buds appeared on the trees. I never ventured out during daylight because I didn't want anyone to see me. I gathered my food at night.

"I had come to love the cottagers. I worked hard at acquiring language, so that I might talk to them. I made rapid progress. Within two months I understood most of the words that the cottagers commonly used. Every conversation of the cottagers now opened new wonders to me.

"What was I? I was ignorant of my creation and creator. I was bigger and stronger than humans. I never had seen anyone who looked like me. Was I, then, some monster?

"Sometimes I wished that I had no thoughts or feelings. I learned that the only way to avoid all pain was to die.

"I learned that there are two sexes, that children are born and grow, that parents love their children, and that humans have friends. Where were *my* family and friends? No parent ever had shown *me* love. I had no memory of growing from small to large. If I died, no one would care. I was alone. Why?

"Soon after my arrival in the hovel, I had discovered some papers in the pocket of the jacket that I had taken from your apartment. At first I had ignored them. After learning to read, I looked through them. The papers were your journal of the four months before my creation. You described every detail of the disgusting work that resulted in my creation. I sickened as I read. 'Hateful day when I received life!' I thought. 'Accursed creator! Why did you form a monster so hideous that even you turned from me in disgust?' You had cruelly abandoned me.

"I hoped that—unlike you—the cottagers would have compassion for me and overlook my appearance. For a few months longer, I practiced speaking. Autumn passed. With surprise and grief, I saw the leaves fall and decay. Nature again assumed a bleak, barren appearance. I saw that the cottagers were kind and generous to beggars who stopped at their door. This increased my hope that they would be kind to me as well.

"When a year had passed since I arrived at the hovel, I decided to delay no longer. I would enter the cottage when the old man was alone. His blindness would prevent him from feeling horror. I would have a chance to talk to him and gain his sympathy.

"One day, when the old man was alone, I fearfully knocked on the cottage door.

"'Come in,' the old man said.

"I entered. 'Pardon this intrusion,' I said. 'I'm a traveler in want of a little rest. You would greatly oblige me if you would allow me to remain in front of the fire for a few minutes.'

"'By all means,' the old man said. 'I'm blind, but I'll do my best to assist you. Would you like some food?'

"I said, 'Don't trouble yourself, kind host. I have food. All I need is warmth and rest.'

"I sat down, and silence followed. I knew that every minute was precious, but I didn't know how to begin. Finally, I said, 'I have no relatives or friends, but I don't want to be alone. I seek human friendship.'"

"'To be friendless is indeed to be unfortunate,' he said. 'But don't despair. People's hearts are full of love and charity.'

"I said, 'I have a good character. I never have harmed anyone. But when people see me, they regard me as a monster rather than a kind friend.'

"With his first trace of fear, the old man asked, 'Why is that?'

"'I'm extremely ugly,' I said.

"With some relief, the old man said, 'Oh! No one should judge you by your physical appearance. I'm blind, so it certainly makes no difference to *me*. You strike me as honorable and sincere. I require good character in a friend, not good looks.'

"'Oh, thank you!' I exclaimed with joy, seizing his hand in gratitude and affection.

"At that instant the cottage door opened, and Felix and Agatha entered. At the sight of me, Agatha fainted. Felix tore me from his father, threw me to the ground, and started beating me with a stick. Because of my superior strength, I easily could have ripped him apart. Instead, I fled into my hovel.

"When night came, I hurried into the woods, where I howled with grief and rage. The stars shone in mockery. The bare trees waved their branches above me. In despair, I sank onto the damp grass. Was there no human who would pity or help me?

"After my usual nightly search for food, I returned to my hovel. The next day, I looked through my chink and saw that the cottage was empty. Its inhabitants had fled, taking all their possessions with them.

"I felt despair, then hatred. If humans were going to treat me like an enemy, I would *be* an enemy. I wanted revenge on them, especially on *you*, my heartless creator. Your journal had told me your name and home city. I resolved to go to Geneva and find you. You had endowed me with feelings and then left me helpless. As my creator, you owed me pity and redress.

"My travels were long and hard. Rain and snow assailed me. Mighty rivers were frozen. The earth's surface was hard, bare, and chill. Usually I traveled only at night, fearful of encountering a human. However, one morning after spring had come, I ventured to travel through deep woods during daylight.

"When I emerged from the woods at the banks of a turbulent river, a young girl came running, in play, toward the spot where I was concealed. At the river's edge, she slipped and fell into the water. I rushed from my hiding place and, struggling against the current, pulled her to shore. She was unconscious but alive. A man emerged from the woods and darted toward me. He tore the girl from my arms and hurried into the woods. Eager to know that the girl was all right, I followed. The man turned, aimed a gun at me, and fired. I fell, wounded, and the man continued on his flight.

"This, then, was the reward for my kindness! I had saved a child and, in return, I had been shot. The shot had shattered flesh and bone in my shoulder. The pain was so intense that I fainted.

"For some weeks I led a miserable life in the woods. In addition to the pain caused by my wound, I felt intense anger at the injustice of my treatment. I hated humans and, once again, vowed revenge on them, especially on my creator. After some weeks my wound healed, and I continued my journey.

"Two months later, I arrived in the area of Geneva. I was awakened from a light sleep by the approach of a young boy, who came playfully running past my hiding place. I thought that, because he was so young, he might not be prejudiced against an ugly creature. I desired to be his friend. Urged by this impulse, I grabbed him as he passed and hugged him. As soon as he saw me, he covered his eyes with his hands and screamed. I drew his hands from his face and said, 'I don't intend to hurt you. Listen to me.'

"He struggled violently. 'Let me go!' he screamed. 'Monster! You want to tear me to pieces and eat me. Hideous monster! My father is Alphonse Frankenstein. If you hurt me, he'll punish you.'

"I thought, 'Frankenstein! You're the kin of my sworn enemy!'

"The child still struggled and hurled abuse at me. I grasped his throat to silence him. In a moment he lay dead at my feet.

"I gazed on my victim. Instead of regret, I felt joy and triumph. 'Like humans, I can destroy!' I thought. 'I'm not simply their help-less victim. This death will cause Victor Frankenstein much-deserved misery.'

"For some days I haunted the spot where I had killed the boy, sometimes wishing to see you, sometimes resolved to kill myself. At length I wandered toward these mountains.

"You alone can satisfy my burning passion. You must comply with my request. I'm alone and miserable. Humans won't associate with me. You must create a female who is like me, so that I can live with her and have the companionship that I need. Only you can do this. I demand it of you as a right. You owe me at least that much."

"I refuse!" Victor said. "You killed my brother. I'm not going to create another crea-ture who will cause harm. Go away! I'll never consent to your demand."

"Who are you to judge me for causing harm?" the creature responded angrily. "You created me and then accepted no responsibility. If anyone is to blame, it's you. What kindness and justice have *you* shown? You would love to do away with me. *You're* the one with murder-ous thoughts. And why should I respect humans, who have treated me so cruelly and unjustly? If you and other humans treated me kindly, I would return the kindness a hundred-fold. If, however, you continue to show me nothing but injustice, I'll have my revenge. What I ask of you is reasonable: a female who will love me, and whom I will love in return. Although we'll be cut off from the rest of the world, we'll have each other. We'll be harmless. Show me this one kindness!"

Victor was moved. He realized that there was justice in the creature's words. As the creature's creator, didn't he owe him some happiness?

"If you agree, I promise that you'll never see me again," the creature continued. "I'll go to a remote part of South America. Unlike humans, I don't kill animals to glut my appetite. I eat vegetable foods such as acorns and berries. My companion, too, will be a peaceful vegetarian, causing harm to no one."

"You propose," Victor said, "to live in exile from humans. Will you really be content with that?"

"I promise you that my companion and I will avoid humans. Free of their evil influence, we'll be entirely peaceful."

Victor felt some compassion, but the creature's hideousness continued to fill him with loathing. "Why should I trust you? You've already shown that you're capable of murder."

"My violence was a reaction to solitude,

misery, and injustice. In contrast, the humans who have been violent toward *me* have acted without cause."

Victor considered all of the creature's arguments and decided that he should comply with his request. "Very well. I'll create a female companion for you if you solemnly swear to leave Europe forever and stay away from humans."

"I swear," the creature said. "Set to work on my companion. I'll be watching and waiting." And he left, descending the mountain more swiftly than an eagle flies.

Victor returned home with a heavy heart, determined to do as he had promised. However, weeks passed without his being able to bring himself to begin the loathsome task. The more he put his promise out of his mind, the better he felt. His health and spirits improved.

One day his father said, "Victor, I'm happy to see that you seem to have recovered from grief. I've always hoped that you and Elizabeth would marry. You've been attached to each other from infancy. You've always seemed entirely suited to each other in tastes and temperament. Do you view her as a sister, or would you rejoice to marry her?"

"Father," Victor replied, "I love Elizabeth with all my heart and completely desire to marry her."

Alphonse was delighted. "Do you wish the wedding to be as soon as possible?" he asked eagerly.

Victor wanted to say "Yes!" but he thought of his unfulfilled promise and the harm that the creature might cause to his family if angered. He realized that he must keep his promise and allow the creature to depart with his bride before he himself could marry. Because he feared for his family and didn't want to begin the gruesome task of creating another monster in his father's house, Victor decided that he must go away to create the creature's mate. "Before marrying Elizabeth, I wish to go to Scotland for some months, on business relating to my scientific interests," Victor told his father.

Alphonse consented. He suggested that Henry accompany Victor. Victor happily agreed, glad to have Henry's company, which might also discourage the creature from confronting him.

It was arranged, then, that Victor would go to Scotland and marry Elizabeth as soon as he returned. One fear haunted Victor: what if the creature took revenge on his family while he was away? The creature, however, had said that he would watch Victor until the promise was fulfilled, and Victor believed this. Also, if the creature hurt Elizabeth or his father, he never would comply with the creature's demand.

At the end of September, Elizabeth bade Victor a tearful goodbye.

As always, Henry provided delightful, cheerful company. In February, Victor and Henry arrived in Scotland.

In Edinburgh, a city known for its medical knowledge, Victor began to collect the information and materials necessary for his new act of creation.

After spending some months in Edinburgh, Victor and Henry received a letter from an acquaintance in Scotland's highlands who had formerly been the Frankensteins' guest in Geneva. He mentioned the beauties of his area and asked Victor and Henry if they would visit. Victor and Henry said yes.

However, as Victor and Henry approached the man's home, Victor told his friend to go on alone. "I'd like to continue touring Scotland alone for a while," Victor said.

"I'd rather stay with you," Henry said, disappointed, "but I'll do as you wish."

Victor believed that the creature must be following him and would reveal himself when the new act of creation was done. He headed to a remote Scottish island, where he could finish his work in solitude.

About five miles from the Scottish mainland,

the island was a place suited to Victor's dark task. It was hardly more than a rocky cliff continually beaten by the waves. The barren soil provided barely enough pasture for the island's few miserable cows. The island's five thin humans ate little more than oatmeal. Bread, vegetables, and even fresh drinking water were luxuries that had to be obtained from the mainland.

The only dwellings on the whole island were three squalid huts. One of these was vacant, so Victor rented it. It contained only two rooms. The thatch had fallen in, the walls were unplastered, and the door was off its hinges. Victor ordered repairs, bought some furniture, and took possession. The island's other residents largely ignored him.

Victor worked irregularly: sometimes only in the morning, sometimes not at all for several days, sometimes throughout the day and night. Alone, engaged in a loathsome task, and fearing that the creature might confront him at any moment, Victor was nervous and depressed.

One evening, as he sat in his laboratory, he had a horrible thought. What if the creature he was about to create proved more harmful than the one he already had created? What if she delighted in causing harm? The already-created creature had sworn to avoid humans, but the yet-unborn creature hadn't. She might refuse to comply with an agreement in which she had no part. She and the creature might even hate each other. The creature loathed his own deformity. Might he not loathe hers as well? Also, she might loathe his. She might turn from him in disgust, desiring a man. She might abandon him. Alone again, he would return to rage.

Even if they went to remote regions, wouldn't they produce offspring? Couldn't this new species become a scourge to humans? Victor wondered if he had the right to take this risk. He had been moved by the creature's arguments and frightened by his threats, but shouldn't he put others' welfare first? He shuddered to think that his actions might place future generations of humans in danger.

When Victor looked up, he saw, by the light of the moon, the creature outside his window. The creature grinned as he gazed on Victor. Victor found the grin ghastly. He thought, "Yes, he has followed me." Trembling with passion, Victor tore to pieces the thing that he was creating.

Seeing the destruction of his one chance for happiness, the creature howled with rage and despair. Within moments, he entered the hut and approached Victor. In a smothered voice, he said, "You have destroyed the work that you began. Do you dare to destroy my hopes? I've hidden in forests, caves, and shelterless heaths. I've endured hunger, cold, and exhaustion. Do you dare to break your promise?"

"I *do* break my promise. I'll never create another being like you, wicked and deformed."

"I reasoned and pleaded with you, but you've shown yourself unworthy. Shall humans and other animals find mates and I alone have no companion? I felt affection, but I've been treated with hatred and scorn. Are you to be happy while I grovel in wretchedness? Tyrant and tormentor, I'll have revenge! You'll regret the suffering that you've inflicted on me."

"Go!"

"I'll go for now, but I'll see you again on your wedding night."

The creature left, but his words continued to ring in Victor's ears. Victor thought, "Why didn't I kill him? Who will be his next victim? Does he intend to kill me on my wedding night? Far more horrible thought—does he intend to kill Elizabeth? I'll kill him first."

The next day, Victor left the island. When he arrived on the mainland, he heard news of a murder committed the previous night. The body of a man in his twenties had been found on the shore. It bore no signs of violence except black finger marks on the neck. The man had been strangled.

Recalling William's murder, Victor trembled with fear and horror. His horror increased when he learned that the murder victim was Swiss. Telling the authorities that he might recognize a fellow Swiss traveling in Scotland, he asked to see the body. Victor entered the room where the corpse lay and was led up to the coffin. Stretched before him was Henry's lifeless body.

Victor gasped for breath. He threw himself onto the body and sobbed. "Henry! No! Oh God, no!" Could his dear friend, so full of life and goodness, really be dead? Victor wished that he had been killed instead. Why did he continue to live? "Death snatches away many blooming, innocent children, the only hopes of their doting parents," he thought. "Why do I live on?"

Victor would have killed himself if he hadn't felt such sharp fear for Elizabeth and his father. If the creature had killed Henry—and he must be the murderer—did he plan to kill Elizabeth and his father next? He must return home as quickly as possible.

When Victor arrived home, Elizabeth greeted him with joy. But she was worried by how thin, haggard, and troubled he looked. Victor conveyed the news that Henry had been murdered.

Even so, the wedding date was set for ten days later. Victor was determined to either kill the creature when he showed himself or be killed by him. He no longer wished to prolong the ordeal. In case the creature attacked him, he started carrying a pistol and a dagger. He always was on the alert.

Elizabeth had inherited a villa on the shore of a nearby lake. It was agreed that she and Victor would live there after their wedding.

Elizabeth seemed happy. Victor's father was overjoyed. The ceremony took place and, after it, a large party at the Frankenstein house. That same day, Elizabeth and Victor departed for the villa. They arrived as night was falling.

Suddenly a storm of rain descended. Victor was fearful and watchful. He had a pistol in his jacket pocket.

Elizabeth noticed his terror. "Victor, what is it that you fear?"

"Nothing, my love. The storm has me on edge." To protect Elizabeth, he told her that she should go to bed. Looking surprised and unhappy, she complied.

Victor searched the house for the creature, looking in every corner in which the creature might hide. There was no sign of him. Suddenly he heard a dreadful scream. It came from Elizabeth's room. Victor rushed to the room as another scream tore the air.

Elizabeth lay dead on the bed, her face pale and distorted. Servants rushed in and observed her body with horror. The mark of the creature's grasp was on her neck.

Victor looked up at the open window and saw the creature, who grinned. Drawing his pistol from his pocket, Victor rushed toward the creature and fired. But the creature escaped unwounded.

Victor and the servants tracked the creature to the lake and pursued him with boats but didn't find him. All the people in the area of the villa were summoned to search for the murderer. Victor himself searched until he was overcome by exhaustion and grief. Then he thought of his father. He might be the next victim!

Weeping all the way, Victor hurried back to Geneva. His father was still alive, but he collapsed at the news of Elizabeth's murder. He had loved her as a daughter. He was unable to rise from his bed. In a few days he died in Victor's arms.

Victor was nearly insane with grief and rage. The only thing that kept him alive was his desire to see the creature dead.

One night Victor visited the graveyard where William, Elizabeth, and his father were buried. Everything was silent except the leaves of the trees, which were gently agitated by the wind. The night was nearly dark. The spirits of the departed seemed to flit around and cast a shadow, which was felt but not seen. Victor said out loud, "I'll pursue the demon who has caused this misery until either he is dead or I am. I'll continue to live in order to carry out this revenge. Spirits of the dead, assist me. Let the accursed and hellish monster feel the despair that now torments me."

Victor heard a loud, fiendish laugh. Then the creature said, "I'm satisfied, miserable wretch! Live on and suffer."

Victor darted toward the spot from which the sound had proceeded. Suddenly moonlight shone on the creature's ghastly, distorted shape. But the creature fled too quickly for Victor to pursue him.

Hoping to find the creature, Victor started to search in desolate regions. Every so often, the creature would leave Victor some clue as to his whereabouts, such as a mark cut into stone or tree bark. These clues were intended to torment Victor and drive him on, so that he wouldn't kill himself and thereby end his suffering. Sometimes Victor would see the creature's huge footprint in the snow.

Victor suffered from cold, want, and exhaustion. Often he survived by killing animals and eating their remains. His life was hateful to him.

One time, the creature left this message: "Now I'm the master; you're the slave. Follow me to the icy north, where you'll suffer from cold and frost, which do not harm me. You'll endure many hard, miserable hours before we fight to the death."

So Victor headed north. The snows thickened, and the cold increased. The peasants were shut up in their hovels. Only a few ventured out to kill animals. The rivers were covered with ice, so Victor couldn't eat any fish, as he usually did.

The creature's triumph increased with Victor's suffering. One message that the creature left stated, "Wrap yourself in fur and bring food. You're going to travel to a place where your sufferings will increase a thousandfold."

Victor resolved not to fail in his purpose. He bought a sled and dogs and traversed wastelands of ice. When he arrived at one Arctic village, the villagers said that a gigantic monster had arrived the night before, armed with a gun. He had entered a solitary cottage, causing the inhabitants to flee, and carried off their store of winter food, placing it in a sled drawn by dogs. He had set off in a direction that led not to land but to floating ice.

On hearing this, Victor at first despaired.

The creature had escaped him. Victor thought, "Surely I'll die if I try to pursue him any further." Then, however, his desire to destroy the creature proved stronger than his fear. He exchanged his land sled for one built to travel over ice floes. He bought lots of provisions and left land.

Immense, rugged mountains of ice often barred his way. He often heard the thunder of breaking ice, which threatened his destruction. But then the water would refreeze, once again allowing him passage. After the sled dogs struggled up the slopes of one icy mountain, one of them died from exhaustion. Victor viewed the icy expanse before him. Then a dark speck on the dusky plain caught his eye. When he recognized the creature in his sled, he cried out with joy. He removed the dead dog from the sled, gave the other dogs a large amount of food, and, after a necessary hour of rest, traveled on. The creature's sled still was visible. Victor gained on it. After two days, his enemy was only about a mile ahead of him.

But now Victor lost all trace of the creature. The sea groaned with breaking ice. The threatening waters rolled and swelled beneath him. The wind rose; the sea roared; and, as with an earthquake's mighty shock, the ice split. Within a few minutes a tumultuous sea rolled between

Victor and his enemy, and he was left drifting on a continually shrinking piece of ice.

Many appalling hours passed. Several of Victor's dogs died. Then Victor saw an anchored ship. He quickly destroyed part of his sled to construct oars, with which he moved his raft of ice toward the ship.

The crew, who were English, took Victor onboard. The entire crew was in danger; at every moment, mountains of ice threatened to crush their ship. Many crew members already had died from the intense cold. The next day, the ice cracked and split in every direction. Two days later, however, the passage south became free. When the sailors saw this, they shouted with joy.

Victor was so weak that he had been bedridden since being taken onboard. He was dying. He no longer felt a desire for revenge. He realized that he should have tried to bestow some happiness on the creature he had created but that he had been right to refuse to create another such creature. With these thoughts uppermost in his mind, Victor died.

Soon after, the creature secretly entered Victor's cabin and sobbed by his coffin. "He was my victim, too," the creature thought. "I destroyed him by destroying everyone he loved. Even as I committed each evil, I suffered from grief and remorse. My heart was shaped to feel love and sympathy. I was wrenched, by misery, to vice and hatred. After I murdered Clerval, I hated myself. I returned to Switzerland feeling pity for Frankenstein. But he, the author of my existence and its unspeakable torments, sought his own enjoyment while denying me any happiness. Once, I had hoped to meet with beings who would overlook my appearance and love me for my excellent qualities. No one did. I've always been alone. I've never known any comfort or companionship. I desired love and fellowship but was spurned. Humans who treated me unjustly and cruelly were admired and loved by others, but I was hated and abused. I then partook of human evil. Like humans, I murdered the innocent and helpless."

"I'll kill myself," the creature decided. "That alone will end my pain. I'll burn myself to death, so that no one can look at my body and make another such creature. When I was new to the world, I delighted in the rustling of leaves and the warbling of birds. I would have wept to die. Now, however, death is my only consolation."

The creature sprang through the cabin window and onto an ice raft that floated close to the ship. And the waves carried him away.

The Strange Case of
DR. JEKYLL
AND
MR. HYDE

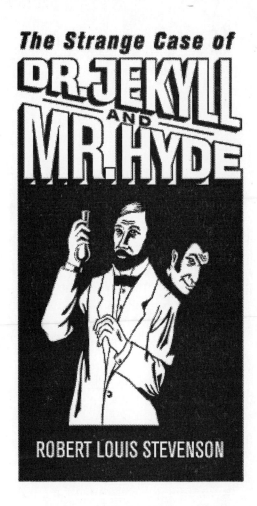

ROBERT LOUIS STEVENSON

Edited, and with an Afterword,
by Joan Dunayer

CONTENTS

CHAPTER 1

Story of the Door

*While out walking, London lawyer Gabriel
Utterson and his cousin Richard Enfield pass a
house occupied by a strange, evil man named
Edward Hyde.*

Gabriel J. Utterson, a London lawyer, had a
rugged face that never was lit by a smile. An
unemotional bachelor, he was reserved and brief
in his speech. He was tall, slender, dusty, and
dreary, yet somehow lovable. At a gathering of
friends, and when the wine suited his taste,
something highly human shone from his eyes—
something that never found its way into his talk
but showed in his after-dinner face and, more
often and clearly, in his actions. He was austere
with himself. When he was alone, he drank gin
rather than wine, which he preferred. Although
he enjoyed theater, he hadn't gone to a theater
for twenty years.

Nevertheless, Utterson's attitude toward others was tolerant, even approving. Sometimes he marveled, almost with envy, at the high spirits with which others indulged themselves. When others were in trouble, he was inclined to help rather than scold. "I let others go to the devil in their own way," he would say. Because he was so tolerant of others' faults, he frequently was the last respectable acquaintance of men of deteriorating character and condition, and the last good influence on them. As long as such men came to his home, his manner toward them remained the same. No doubt, this unchanged manner was easy for Utterson because he rarely showed emotion.

Utterson's friendship was largely a product of his good nature. Usually, modest people accept as friends those with whom they simply become acquainted, and that was Utterson's way. His friends were his relatives and other people whom he had known the longest. Like ivy, his affections grew over time. They didn't indicate any merit in those he befriended.

Utterson had a bond with his distant cousin Richard Enfield, a younger, well-known man about town. Many people couldn't understand what Utterson and Enfield saw in each other or what interests they shared. People who saw Utterson and Enfield on their Sunday walks together reported that the two said nothing, looked bored, and would greet the appearance of a friend with obvious relief. Nevertheless, Utterson and Enfield greatly valued their walks together; to enjoy those walks uninterrupted, they would forego opportunities for business or pleasure.

On one of their walks, Utterson and Enfield happened to stroll down a small side street that was busy with trade on weekdays but quiet on Sundays. The street's residents were successful and ambitious. The shops, their goods displayed in the front window, had an inviting air, like rows of smiling salespeople. Even on Sundays, when it was largely empty of pedestrians, the street shone out in contrast to its dingy neighborhood. With its freshly painted shutters, well-polished brass fixtures, and general cleanliness and gaiety, the street caught and pleased a pedestrian's eyes.

Two doors from one corner was a sinister, block-shaped building two stories high. Windowless, it showed nothing but a door on the lower story and a blank, discolored wall on the upper. In every feature, it bore the marks of prolonged neglect. The door, which had neither a bell nor a knocker, was blistered and stained. Tramps slouched in the recess and struck matches on the panels; children kept shop on the steps; someone had carelessly jabbed at the moldings with a knife. For a generation, no one had appeared to drive away these random visitors or repair their vandalism.

When Utterson and Enfield were across from the house's door, Enfield lifted his cane and pointed. "Did you ever notice that door?"

"Yes," Utterson said.

"It calls to mind a very odd story."

"Indeed?" Utterson said, with a slight change of tone. "What story?"

"Well, it was this way," Enfield said. "About three o'clock one black winter morning, I was returning home from distant travels. My way took me through a part of town where nothing but street lamps were visible. Street after empty street, all the residents were asleep. I started to feel tense, started listening intently and longing for the sight of a police officer. Suddenly I saw two people. One was a small man hurrying along. The other was a girl about nine years old who was running down a cross street. The two ran into each other at the corner.

"Then came the horrible part. The man calmly trampled the child and left her screaming on the ground. He seemed inhuman, like some force that crushes everything in its path. I gave a few shouts, ran after him, collared him, and brought him back to where a group of people had gathered around the screaming child. The man was perfectly cool and didn't resist. But he gave me such a hateful look that it made me sweat.

"The people who had gathered were the girl's family. Pretty soon, the doctor who had been summoned arrived at the scene. He said that the child was fine except badly frightened.

"You might think that the incident would have ended there. However, I had taken an instant, intense dislike to the man who had trampled the girl. So had her family, as was natural. But it was the doctor's reaction that especially struck me. He was a typical physician, of nondescript age and complexion, with a strong Scottish accent and unemotional manner. Yet, every time he looked at my prisoner, his face whitened and showed a desire to kill him. I felt the same desire.

"Because killing was out of the question, the doctor and I told the man that we would make such a scandal out of this that his name would stink from one end of London to the other. If he had any respectable friends or positive reputation, we would see that he lost them.

"As we spoke in red-hot anger, we did our best to keep the women off him. They were wild with anger and circled the man.

"Although he was visibly frightened, he displayed a devilish sneering coolness. 'If you choose to make much of this accident,' he said, 'I'm helpless to stop you. Like any other gentleman, I wish to avoid a scene. Name your price.'

"We got him to agree to give the child's family a hundred pounds. He led us to the very door you see across the street. He whipped out a key, went in, and quickly returned with ten pounds in gold and a check for ninety more. The check bore the signature of a highly respected, well-known man.

"'I doubt that the check is genuine,' I said to the man. 'A man doesn't walk into a house at 4 a.m. and come out with another man's check for nearly a hundred pounds.'

"But he sneered, 'Set your mind at rest. I'll stay with you until the bank opens and cash the check myself.'

"The man, the doctor, the child's father, and I spent the rest of the night at my house. The next morning, after we had eaten breakfast, we all went to the bank. I handed over the check and said that I believed it to be a forgery. To my great surprise, the check was genuine."

"Oh my!" Utterson said.

"I see you feel as I do," Enfield said. "Yes, it's a bad story. The man was someone whom respected people should shun. He really was damnable. Yet, the person who had signed the check was regarded as honorable and kind. I assume he wrote the check because he was being blackmailed. He must have been an honest man who was paying heavily for some misdeed committed when he was young."

"Do you know if the provider of the check lives here?" Utterson asked.

"I don't know," Enfield said.

"You never asked?"

"No. I didn't want to intrude or damage his reputation. But I've looked around the place. There isn't any other door. No one goes in or out except, on rare occasion, the man who trampled the child. The first floor has no windows. Three second-floor windows face the courtyard. They're clean but always shut. The chimney usually is smoking, so someone must live there."

For a time, the pair walked on in silence. Then Utterson said, "What's the name of the man who trampled the child?"

"Well, I guess it wouldn't do any harm to say. His name is Edward Hyde."

"What does he look like?"

"He isn't easy to describe. There's something wrong with his appearance, something downright detestable. I never saw a man I so disliked, yet I scarcely know why. He must be deformed, although I can't say in what way."

After walking some way in silence, Utterson asked, "You're sure that he used a key? I ask because . . . well, I know the name of the man who must have signed the check."

"You should have told me that you knew," Enfield said, annoyed. "Hyde had a key. What's more, he still has it. I saw him use it less than a week ago."

CHAPTER 2

Search for Mr. Hyde

In his will, Utterson's friend Dr. Henry Jekyll has left all of his possessions to Hyde. Wondering why, Utterson goes out of his way to meet Hyde.

That evening Utterson returned home feeling somber. He ate his dinner without relish. It was his custom on Sundays, when his meal was over, to sit by the fire, reading some dry religious book, until the clock of the nearby church rang out the hour of midnight, when he would go soberly and gratefully to bed. However, on this night, right after dinner, he took up a candle and went into his office. There he opened his safe and removed a document identified on its envelope as the will of Henry Jekyll, a doctor of medicine and law and a member of a prestigious science organization, the Royal Society.

With a troubled expression, Utterson sat down to study the will, entirely handwritten by Jekyll. It stated that, in the event of Jekyll's death, all of Jekyll's possessions should go to his "friend and benefactor Edward Hyde." It also stated that, in the event of Jekyll's "disappearance or unexplained absence" of more than three months, Hyde should step into Jekyll's shoes, free of any burden or obligation other than to pay a few small sums to members of the doctor's household.

This document had bothered Utterson for a long time. It offended him both as a lawyer and as someone who greatly valued the normal and customary. Now that Hyde seemed detestable, the will bothered him even more. "Before I thought the will was crazy," he thought as he returned it to the safe. "Now I fear it's also a disgrace."

Utterson blew out his candle, put on a coat, and headed toward Cavendish Square, where his friend Dr. Hastie Lanyon lived and received his many patients. "If anyone can explain this mystery, it's Lanyon," he thought.

Lanyon's solemn butler recognized and welcomed Utterson and led him directly into the dining room. Lanyon sat alone drinking wine. He was a robust, elegantly dressed, red-faced gentleman with thick, prematurely white hair and a boisterous, decisive manner.

Upon seeing Utterson, Lanyon sprang up from his chair and welcomed him with both hands. Lanyon's warmth, although it appeared somewhat theatrical, was based on genuine feeling. Utterson and Lanyon were old friends. They had been classmates in high school and college. Both thoroughly respected themselves and each other. They also thoroughly enjoyed each other's company.

After some rambling talk, Utterson led up to the subject with which he was so disagreeably preoccupied. "I suppose," he said, "you and I must be Henry Jekyll's two oldest friends."

"I wish we were, instead, his youngest friends," Lanyon joked. "I suppose we *are* his oldest friends. Still, I see little of him now."

"Indeed? I thought the two of you must often discuss medicine."

"We used to. For more than ten years now, Jekyll has had ideas that are too strange for my taste. He's become mentally unsound, given to unscientific nonsense." Lanyon flushed with disapproval.

Utterson thought, *Oh, Lanyon and Jekyll have disagreed about some scientific matter.* After giving Lanyon some time to regain his composure, he asked, "Have you ever met an acquaintance of Jekyll's named Hyde?"

"No. Never heard of him," Lanyon answered.

Utterson went home having obtained no further information. After going to bed, he tossed and turned throughout the night. He pictured the lit lamps of an otherwise dark and empty London side street, a man walking swiftly, a running child, the collision of the two, the man trampling the child and hurrying on despite her screams. Then he pictured an elegant bedroom in which Jekyll lay sleeping and smiling at pleasant dreams: the door of the bedroom opened and a man pushed the bed curtains aside, standing by Jekyll, exerting power over him; Jekyll rose to do the man's bidding. The powerful figure haunted Utterson all night. When he managed to doze off, he imagined it gliding secretively through houses with sleeping occupants or moving more and more swiftly through ever-wider mazes of a lamp-lit city, crushing a child at every street corner and leaving her screaming. The figure had no familiar face. Whenever features would start to take shape, they then would melt away. When the bells of the nearby church chimed 6 a.m., Utterson still was thinking about the story that Enfield had told him.

Utterson developed an intense desire to see Hyde's actual features. If he could see Hyde, he thought, the mystery would lessen and not burden him so much. He might discover the reason for Jekyll's strange association with Hyde. Hyde's face would be worth seeing: the face of a man without pity, a face that aroused loathing in Enfield and others who saw it.

From then on, Utterson haunted the door in the side street of shops. Each morning before his office hours, at noon when business was brisk and time scarce, at night under the fog-shrouded moon, by all lights and at all hours, he kept watch.

"If he's Hyde, I'll be Seek," Utterson joked to himself.

One dry, frosty night, Utterson's patience finally was rewarded. The streets were as clean as a ballroom floor. Unshaken by any wind, the street lamps drew a regular pattern of light and shadow. By 10 p.m. the shops were closed and the side street was empty and silent. Small sounds carried far. Domestic sounds from inside the houses were audible on either side of the street. The approach of any pedestrian was heard long before the person arrived. Utterson had been at his post for some minutes when he became aware of an odd, light footstep drawing near. During his nightly watches, he had grown accustomed to hearing an individual's footsteps first at a distance, then suddenly standing out distinctly from the city's background hum and clatter. However, never before had his attention been so sharply arrested. Sensing success, he concealed himself in the courtyard's entryway.

The steps swiftly approached. They swelled out suddenly louder as they turned the end of the street. Looking out from his hiding place, Utterson saw the type of man with whom he was dealing. The man was small, plainly dressed, and somehow—even at a distance—repulsive. He made straight for the door, crossing the street to save time. As he came, he drew a key from his pocket.

Utterson stepped out and touched him on the shoulder as he passed. "Mr. Hyde, I think?"

Hyde shrank back, sucking in his breath with a hiss. But his fear was only momentary. Although he didn't look Utterson in the face, he said coolly, "That's my name. What do you want?"

"I see you're going in," Utterson replied. "I'm Mr. Utterson, an old friend of Dr. Jekyll. You must have heard him mention me. Meeting you so conveniently, I thought I might enter the house with you."

"Dr. Jekyll isn't here," Hyde said.

He and Utterson stared at each other for a few seconds.

"It's good that we've met," Hyde said.

ITEM CHARGED

LIB#: *1000221232*
GRP: STUDENT

Due: 10/16/2013 08:00 PM

Title: Frankenstein / Mary Wollstonecraft
Shelley ; edited, and with an afterword,
by Joan Dunayer. The strange case of
Dr. Jekyll and Mr. Hyde / Robert Louis
Stevenson ; edited, and with an
afterword by Joan Dunayer.
Auth: Shelley, Mary Wollstonecraft,
1797-1851.
Call #: 428.64 SHELLY 2005
Enum
Chron
Copy: 2
Item *0072533K*

"You should have my address." He told Utterson a Soho address.

"Good God!" Utterson thought. "Does he want me to have his address because he's thinking about Jekyll's will?"

"How did you know me?" Hyde asked.

"By description," Utterson replied.

"Whose description?"

"We have friends in common," Utterson said.

"Friends in common," Hyde echoed, somewhat hoarsely. "Who?"

"Jekyll, for instance."

"He never told you!" Hyde cried, with a flash of anger. "I didn't think you would lie."

"Come now," Utterson objected. "That isn't suitable language."

Hyde snarled and then laughed savagely. The next moment, with extraordinary quickness, he had unlocked the door and disappeared inside.

Upset, Utterson stood there awhile. Then he slowly walked away, pausing every few steps and putting his hand to his brow in confusion. Hyde was pale and dwarfish. As Enfield had said, he gave an impression of deformity without having any identifiable deformity. He had a displeasing smile. He had shown a murderous combination of timidity and boldness. He spoke with a husky, whispering, somewhat broken voice. Utterson felt a previously unknown disgust, loathing, and fear. *The man hardly seems human*, he thought. *He seems like some sort of cave-dweller, some throwback to the pre-human. Is it that he radiates evil? I think so. Poor Henry Jekyll. If ever I read Satan's signature on a face, that signature is on Hyde's.*

Around the corner from the side street, there was a square of old, handsome houses. Now largely rundown, these houses were rented to all sorts of people: architects, sleazy lawyers, and people involved in shady business practices. However, one house, the second from the corner, still wore an air of wealth and comfort. Utterson stopped and knocked.

A well-dressed, elderly butler opened the door.

"Is Dr. Jekyll at home, Poole?" Utterson asked.

"I will see, Mr. Utterson," Poole said, admitting Utterson into a large, low-ceilinged hall warmed by a bright, open fire and furnished with costly oak cabinets. "Will you wait here by the fire, sir? Or shall I give you a light in the dining room?"

"Here, thank you," Utterson said. He drew near to the fire and leaned against the tall screen in front of it. Jekyll was proud of this hall.

Utterson himself thought it one of the most pleasant rooms in London. Tonight, however, there was a shudder in his blood. Hyde's face sat heavily on his memory. He felt a nausea and distaste of life that were rare for him. Feeling so gloomy, he seemed to read a threat in the firelight's flickering on the polished cabinets and the shadows flitting on the ceiling. He was ashamed of his relief when Poole returned to say that Jekyll had gone out.

"I saw Mr. Hyde enter by Dr. Jekyll's laboratory, Poole," Utterson said. "Is that all right, when Dr. Jekyll isn't home?"

"It's fine, sir," Poole replied. "Mr. Hyde has a key."

"Your master seems to place considerable trust in that young man, Poole," Utterson said.

"Yes, sir, he does," Poole said. "We've been instructed to obey him."

"Why haven't I ever met Mr. Hyde?" Utterson asked.

"He never dines here," Poole replied. "We see very little of him on this side of the house. Mostly, he comes and goes by way of the laboratory."

"Well, goodnight, Poole."

"Goodnight, Mr. Utterson."

Utterson headed home with a heavy heart. *Poor Henry Jekyll,* he thought. *I fear that he's in deep trouble. He was wild when he was young. That was a long time ago, but he must be paying now for some old sin, some long-concealed disgrace.* Frightened by the thought, Utterson brooded awhile on his own past. He groped in all the corners of his memory, trying to determine if he, too, might be guilty of some old sin. No, his past seemed quite blameless. Few men could read the account of their own life with less fear. Yet, he was humbled by the many misdeeds that he had committed. He was raised up again, by gratitude, at the thought of how many more he had come close to committing. Then his thoughts returned to Jekyll. *Things can't continue as they are,* he thought. *It turns me cold to think of this creature stealing like a thief to Henry's bedside. Poor Henry! And the danger of it! If Hyde suspects the existence of the will, he might become impatient to inherit. I have to do something about this if only Henry will let me.*

CHAPTER 3

Dr. Jekyll Was Quite at Ease

Utterson asks Jekyll why Hyde is Jekyll's heir.
Jekyll gives no satisfactory answer.

Two weeks later, Utterson was invited to one of the pleasant dinners that Jekyll periodically gave for a small group of long-time friends, all intelligent, reputable men and good judges of wine. After the others had left, Utterson stayed behind, as he often did at dinners. When people liked Utterson, they liked him a lot. As more lighthearted and talkative men were leaving, hosts loved to ask the dry lawyer to stay a while longer. They liked to sit in his unobtrusive company, practicing for solitude, sobering their minds in his rich silence after the strain of gaiety.

Jekyll was no exception to the rule. He now sat on the opposite side of the fire. He was a large, well-built man of fifty with a smooth face.

Although he was somewhat stylish, he showed every mark of ability and kindness. He felt a sincere, warm affection for Utterson.

"Henry, I've been wanting to speak to you about your will," Utterson said.

Jekyll responded cheerfully, but someone observing him closely might have noticed that he found the topic distasteful. "My poor Gabriel," he said, "you're unfortunate to have me for a client. I've never seen a man as distressed as you were about my will, with the possible exception of Lanyon with regard to what he called my scientific heresies. Oh, you needn't frown. I know that he's a good fellow, an excellent fellow. And I always mean to see more of him. But he's an ignorant pedant. I've never been more disappointed in any man than I am in Lanyon."

"You know I never approved of the will," Utterson said, bringing the conversation back to the topic he wanted to pursue.

"I know," Jekyll said a bit sharply. "You've told me that."

"Well, I'm telling you again," Utterson said. "I've been hearing about young Hyde."

Jekyll's large, handsome face paled—even his lips. "I don't wish to hear more. I thought we agreed to drop this matter."

"What I've heard about Hyde is horrible," Utterson said.

"It can't make any difference. You don't understand my position. I'm in a painful situation, Gabriel. It won't do any good to talk about it."

"Henry, you know me. I'm trustworthy. Tell me, in confidence, what this is about, and I'm certain I can help you."

"That's good of you, Gabriel, and I thank you. I fully believe you. I trust you more than any other man, even more than I trust myself. But the situation isn't as you imagine. It's not as bad as that. Just put your good heart at rest. The moment I choose, I can be rid of Hyde. I give you my word on that. I thank you, but—please don't be offended—this is a private matter. Please say no more about it."

Looking into the fire, Utterson reflected a little. At last he said, "I suppose you're right." He got to his feet.

"There's one point I'd like you to understand," Jekyll said. "I have a great interest in poor Hyde. I know you've seen him. He told me so. I fear he was rude. But I sincerely take a great interest in that young man. I'd like you to promise that, if anything happens to me, you'll bear with him and see that his rights are respected. I think you would do that if you knew the situation. It would be a weight off my mind if you would promise."

"I can't pretend that I'll ever like him," Utterson said.

"I don't ask that," Jekyll pleaded, laying his hand on Utterson's arm. "I ask only for justice. I ask only that you help him, for my sake, when I'm no longer here."

Utterson heaved an involuntary sigh. "Well then, I promise."

CHAPTER 4

The Carew Murder Case

Hyde viciously murders an elderly gentleman.

Nearly a year later, in October 1886, London was shocked by a crime of singular ferocity. The crime was all the more notable in that the victim was someone of high position. The details were few and startling.

A maid living alone in a house not far from the river had gone upstairs to bed about eleven. The early part of the night was cloudless; a full moon brilliantly lit the lane on which the maid's window looked out. Romantically inclined, she sat down on a chest that stood just under the window and fell into dream-like thoughts. When, with streaming tears, she later reported the incident, she said that she never had felt more at peace or more kindly toward all people. As she sat, she became aware of a handsome, white-haired gentleman coming down the lane. A very small man, to whom she at first paid little attention, advanced to meet the elderly gentleman. When they had come within speaking distance, just under the maid's window, the older man bowed and addressed the other man politely. The topic of conversation didn't appear to be important. The older man sometimes pointed as if asking for directions. The moon shone on his face as he spoke. The maid was pleased to watch it. It seemed to breathe innocence, kindness, nobility, and well-founded self-content. Then her eye wandered to the other man. She was surprised to recognize Mr. Hyde. He once had visited her master, and she had disliked him. He was handling a heavy cane. He never answered a word and seemed to listen with ill-contained impatience. Suddenly he exploded with anger. He stomped with his foot, waved his cane, and carried on like a madman. The elderly gentleman took a step back, looking very surprised and somewhat hurt. Then Hyde struck him to the ground with his cane. With fury, Hyde trampled his victim and struck him again and again. The elderly man's body bounced at the blows and his bones audibly shattered. At the horror of these sights and sounds, the maid fainted.

At 2 a.m. she regained consciousness and

called for the police. The murderer was long gone, but his victim lay—incredibly mangled— in the middle of the lane. Although the cane with which the murder had been committed was of very hard wood, it had broken in half under the violence of this senseless brutality. One splintered half had rolled into a nearby gutter. No doubt, the murderer had carried away the other half. A purse and gold watch were found on the victim, but no cards or papers other than a sealed, stamped envelope addressed to Utterson.

The next day, police inspector Newcomen of Scotland Yard brought this envelope to Utterson's house before Utterson was out of bed. Newcomen told Utterson that Hyde was suspected of murder. "We don't know the victim's identity yet," Newcomen said. "Do you think you might be able to identify the body?"

"Very possibly," Utterson said solemnly. "Please wait while I dress."

Newcomen and Utterson were driven to the police station. As soon as Utterson entered the cell with the body, he nodded. "Yes, I recognize him. I'm sorry to say that this is Sir Danvers Carew."

"Good God, sir!" Newcomen exclaimed. "Is it possible? This will cause quite a stir. Perhaps you can help us find the suspect."

Newcomen narrated what the maid had seen and showed Utterson the broken cane.

Although the cane was battered and broken, Utterson recognized it as one that he himself had given Jekyll many years before. He reflected, then said, "Come with me in my carriage. I'll take you to Hyde's house, in Soho."

By this time it was about 9 a.m. A great brown fog hung like a veil. The wind continually shifted the fog. As the carriage crawled from street to street, the air showed many different colors and degrees of light and dark. Here it was as dark as deep night. There it was a rich, glowing brown, like the light of some strange fire. Here, for a moment, the fog was broken up, so that a thin shaft of daylight shone amid the swirling wreaths.

Under these changing appearances, the dismal, muddy district of Soho, with its dirty inhabitants, was nightmarish in Utterson's eyes. The street lamps were lit, having either been left on or having been re-lit to combat the darkness caused by the fog. Utterson's thoughts were gloomy. When he glanced at Newcomen, sitting beside him, he felt some of that fear of law officers that even the most honest people sometimes feel.

As the carriage drew up to Hyde's residence, the fog lifted a little and revealed a dingy street, a bar, a low-class French restaurant, a shop that sold one- and two-penny salads, ragged children huddled in the doorways, and women of many different nationalities passing by. The next moment, the fog again concealed these squalid surroundings. This was the home of Jekyll's favorite, Hyde, who would inherit a quarter of a million pounds upon Jekyll's death.

An elderly woman with an ivory face and silver hair opened the door. She had an evil face, smoothed by hypocrisy, but her manners were excellent. "Yes, this is Mr. Hyde's residence," she said, "but he isn't home. He came in very late last night but went away again within an hour."

"Don't you find that strange?" Newcomen asked.

"No," she said. "His habits are very irregular. He often is away. Until yesterday, I hadn't seen him for nearly two months."

"Very well, then, we wish to see his rooms," Utterson said.

"That isn't possible. I . . ."

"I'd better tell you," Utterson said. "This is Inspector Newcomen of Scotland Yard."

Repulsive joy flashed across the woman's face. "Ah!" she said. "Mr. Hyde is in trouble! What has he done?"

Utterson   and   Newcomen   exchanged

glances. "He doesn't seem a very popular character," Newcomen said. "Now, my good woman, just let this gentleman and me have a look inside."

The entire house was empty except for two rooms furnished with luxury and good taste. A closet was filled with wine. The dinnerware was silver and the table linen elegant. A fine painting hung on the walls—a gift, Utterson supposed, from Jekyll, who had excellent taste in art. The carpets were thick and of rich color.

At this moment, however, the rooms bore every mark of having been recently and hurriedly ransacked: clothes lay on the floor, with their pockets inside out; drawers were open; a pile of gray ashes lay on the hearth, as though many papers had been burned.

From these ashes Newcomen dug out part of a green checkbook, which had withstood the fire. The missing half of the murder weapon was found behind the door. Because this clinched his suspicions, Newcomen was delighted.

A visit to the bank, where Hyde had an account of several thousand pounds, completed Newcomen's satisfaction. "You may depend on it, sir," Newcomen told Utterson. "I'll soon have Mr. Hyde. He must have lost his head, or he never would have left the cane or burned the checkbook. He'll need money. All that Scotland

Yard has to do is distribute flyers describing him and wait for him to show up at the bank."

However, it wasn't easy to describe Hyde. Few people were familiar with him. The master of the maid who had witnessed the murder had seen Hyde only twice. No one could trace Hyde to any family or find a photo of him. The few people who could describe him differed widely in their descriptions. They all agreed on only one point: Hyde was somehow deformed.

CHAPTER 5

Incident of the Letter

Jekyll gives Utterson a letter signed by Hyde.
The handwriting resembles Jekyll's.

Late in the afternoon, Utterson went to Jekyll's residence. Poole admitted him at once, leading him through the kitchen and across the backyard to what was known as the science building. Jekyll had bought the building from the heirs of a famous surgeon. He used it as a laboratory and office.

This was the first time Utterson had been in the science building. Most of it was a former surgery theater, where medical students had watched physicians dissect cadavers and perform surgery on patients. This round theater filled almost the entire ground floor. It was lit by whatever natural light entered through the windows of its domed roof.

Utterson eyed the dingy, otherwise-window-less theater with curiosity. He had a distasteful sense of strangeness as he crossed the room, which now was silent and desolate, its tables laden with chemical apparatus, its floor strewn with crates and littered with packing straw. Daylight fell dimly through the ceiling's foggy dome.

A hallway joined the surgery theater to the door on the side street. At the same far end as this door, stairs mounted to a door covered with a red felt-like material. Behind this door was an upper story consisting of Jekyll's private laboratory and office.

Proceeding up the stairs and through the doorway, Utterson entered Jekyll's laboratory. It was a large room with, among other things, a tall, free-standing mirror; a desk; and three dusty, iron-barred windows that overlooked the courtyard. A fire burned in the grate. A lit lamp sat on the chimney shelf.

Close to the fire's warmth sat Jekyll, looking deathly ill. He didn't rise to greet Utterson. He just held out a cold hand and welcomed Utterson in a changed voice.

As soon as Poole left, Utterson asked, "Have you heard the news?"

Jekyll shuddered. "The newspaper boys were crying it in the square. I heard them from my dining room."

"Carew was my client, but so are you. I want to know what I should do. You haven't been crazy enough to let Hyde hide here?"

"Gabriel, I swear to God I'll never set eyes on him again. I give you my word of honor. I'm done with him. Indeed, Hyde doesn't want my help. You don't know him as I do. He's safe, quite safe. Mark my words. No one ever will hear of him again."

Utterson listened gloomily. He didn't like his friend's feverish manner. "You seem pretty sure of him. For your sake, I hope you're right. If this matter goes to trial, your name might come up."

"I'm sure of him," Jekyll replied. "I have grounds for certainty that I can't share with any-one. But there is one thing on which you can advise me. I've received a letter from him, and I don't know whether I should show it to the police. I'd like to leave the matter in your hands, Gabriel. You'll judge wisely. I have great trust in you."

"You fear that the letter might lead to Hyde's being found?"

"No. I don't think I care what becomes of Hyde. I was thinking of my own reputation, which this hateful business has jeopardized."

Utterson pondered awhile. He was sur-prised by his friend's selfishness yet somewhat relieved by it. "Well," he said at last, "let me see the letter."

The letter was written in an odd, upright hand and signed "Edward Hyde." The writer stated that he had proved unworthy of Jekyll's many acts of generosity and that Jekyll should feel no alarm about his safety because he had a guaranteed means of escape.

The letter pleased Utterson. It placed the relationship between Jekyll and Hyde in a better light than he had expected. He blamed himself for some of his past suspicions. "Do you have the envelope?" Utterson asked.

"I burned it before I thought about what I was doing," Jekyll said. "It wasn't postmarked. Someone brought it."

"Shall I keep the letter and sleep on the matter?" Utterson asked.

"Yes. I'd like you to judge for me. I've lost confidence in myself."

"Did Hyde dictate the terms of your will?"

Jekyll shut his mouth tightly and nodded.

"I thought so," Utterson said. "I think he intended to murder you. You've had a lucky escape."

"I've learned a lesson," Jekyll said solemnly. "God, what a lesson I've learned!" For a moment he covered his face with his hands.

On his way out, Utterson said to Poole,

"Someone gave you a letter today. What was the messenger like?"

"No, sir," Poole said. "Nothing came today except by post, and there weren't any letters."

This news renewed Utterson's fears. As he walked along, newspaper boys were crying themselves hoarse. "Special edition! Shocking murder of a member of Parliament!" That was the funeral oration for one of his friends and clients. He couldn't help fearing that the good name of another was about to be sucked down in the scandal's whirlpool. He had to make a difficult decision. Although he was self-reliant by habit, he started to long for advice.

Later that day, he sat on one side of his hearth, and Mr. Guest, his chief clerk, sat on the other. Midway between them was a bottle of fine wine from Utterson's wine cellar. Fog still veiled the city, where lamps glimmered like rubies. Muffled by the fog, the business of the city continued, with carriages and pedestrians proceeding along the streets with a wind-like sound. But the room was cheerful with firelight.

There was no man from whom Utterson kept fewer secrets than Guest, and he was not always sure that he kept as many as he had intended to. Guest often went to Jekyll's house on business. He knew Poole. He scarcely could have failed to hear about Hyde's free access to

Jekyll's house. He might have drawn conclusions that cast Jekyll in a negative light. Was it not as well, then, for him to see Hyde's letter? Guest was a man of good sense. He hardly could read the letter without making some remark. That remark might help Utterson decide what to do.

"This is a sad business about Sir Danvers," Utterson said.

"Indeed, sir. It has aroused a great deal of feeling among the public. The killer, of course, was insane."

"I'd like to hear your views on that," Utterson said. "I have a letter here that he wrote. This is just between you and me. I don't know what to do about the letter. This is an ugly business. Here it is: the writing of a murderer."

Guest's eyes widened with interest. He sat down and studied the letter. "The handwriting doesn't look like that of a madman," he said. "But it's peculiar."

Just then a servant entered with a note.

"Is that from Dr. Jekyll, sir?" Guest asked. "I think I recognize his handwriting."

"Yes, it's a dinner invitation. Do you want to see it?"

"Yes, please." Guest laid Hyde's letter and Jekyll's invitation side by side and carefully compared them. "Thank you, sir," he finally said, returning both.

"Why did you compare them, Guest?"

"Well, sir, there's a strong resemblance between Mr. Hyde's and Dr. Jekyll's handwriting. In fact, in many ways they're identical. They just slant differently."

"That's odd," Utterson said.

"Yes."

"Please don't mention this to anyone," Utterson said.

"No, sir. I understand."

As soon as Utterson was alone that night, he locked the letter in his safe. "What?" he thought. "Henry Jekyll forge for a murderer?" His blood ran cold in his veins.

CHAPTER 6

Remarkable Incident of Dr. Lanyon

*Dr. Hastie Lanyon falls ill and dies after a
shocking discovery about Jekyll. A sealed envelope
left by Lanyon instructs Utterson to read the
contents only after Jekyll disappears or dies.*

Thousands of pounds were offered as a reward
for information leading to Hyde's arrest. Sir
Danvers's death was resented as an injury to the
public. But Hyde had disappeared as if he never
had existed. Much of his past was unearthed: all
disreputable. Tales came out about his cruelty,
his vile life, his strange associates, the hatred
that he aroused. But there was no clue as to his
present whereabouts. From the time he had left
the Soho house on the morning of the murder,
he simply had vanished.

As time passed, Utterson began to recover
from his alarm and be more at peace with himself. Hyde and his evil influence were gone.

Jekyll began a new life. He came out of seclusion, renewed friendships, once again was a frequent guest and host, and, although he always had been known for his charity, now was no less distinguished for religion. He kept busy, often was outside, and did good deeds. His consciousness of service caused his face to open and brighten. For more than two months, Jekyll was at peace.

On January 8, Utterson and a few others dined at Jekyll's. Lanyon was there. As in the old days, Utterson, Jekyll, and Lanyon seemed a trio of inseparable friends.

On the 12th and again on the 14th, Utterson was denied admission to Jekyll's house. "The doctor isn't seeing anyone," Poole said.

On the 15th, Utterson tried again but again was refused entry. Having seen his friend almost every day for the last two months, he was deeply troubled by Jekyll's return to solitude.

On the 17th, Utterson went to see Lanyon. He was shocked by the change in Lanyon's appearance. Lanyon seemed near death. The rosy man had grown pale; his flesh had fallen away; he was visibly balder and older. In addition to showing these signs of rapid physical decay, Lanyon seemed terrified. Utterson believed that Lanyon must be fearing death. "He's a doctor," Utterson thought. "He must know that his days are numbered. The knowledge of his approaching death must be more than he can bear."

When Utterson remarked on Lanyon's appearance of illness, Lanyon said plainly, "I've had a shock from which I'll never recover. Within a few weeks, I'll be dead. My life has been pleasant. I've enjoyed it. At least, I used to enjoy it."

"Henry Jekyll also is ill," Utterson said. "Have you seen him?"

Lanyon's face changed. He held up a trembling hand. "I have no wish to see or hear anything more about Jekyll," he said in a loud, unsteady voice. "I'm done with him. I regard him as dead. I beg you to spare me any mention of him."

"What?" Utterson exclaimed. "Is there anything I can do to patch things up between you? You, Henry, and I are three very old friends, Hastie. We won't live to make others."

"Nothing can be done," Lanyon said. "Ask Jekyll."

"He won't see me."

"That doesn't surprise me," Lanyon said bitterly. "Someday, Gabriel, after I'm dead, you might learn what this is all about. I can't tell you. Now, if you can sit and talk with me about other things, for God's sake, stay and do so. But if you can't stay away from this accursed topic, then in God's name, go, because I can't bear it."

As soon as he got home, Utterson sat down and wrote to Jekyll, complaining of his exclusion from Jekyll's house and asking the cause of Jekyll's unhappy break with Lanyon. The next day, Utterson received a long but mysterious letter from Jekyll. The quarrel with Lanyon was incurable. "I don't blame our old friend," Jekyll wrote, "but I share his view that we must never meet again. From now on, I intend to lead a life of extreme seclusion. You mustn't be surprised or doubt my friendship if my door often is shut to you. You must allow me to go my own dark way. I have brought on myself a punishment and danger that I can't name. If I'm the chief of sinners, I'm also the chief of sufferers. I wouldn't have thought that such suffering and terror were possible. You can do only one thing to lighten my burden: respect my silence."

Utterson was amazed. Hyde's dark influence had been withdrawn. Jekyll had returned to his old tasks and friendships. A week ago he had seemed headed for a cheerful, honored old age. Now his friendships, peace of mind, entire life seemed wrecked. Such a sudden and great change pointed to insanity. But Lanyon's manner and words suggested that something else was wrong with Jekyll.

A week later, Lanyon took to his bed. In less than two weeks, he was dead.

With great sadness, Utterson attended Lanyon's funeral. That night, Utterson locked his office door and, sitting by the light of a melancholy candle, took out and set before him an envelope from Lanyon. It was marked, "PRIVATE: for Gabriel J. Utterson ONLY. Should his death precede mine, this should be destroyed unread."

Utterson dreaded looking at the contents. "I buried one friend today," he thought. "What if this costs me another?" Then he broke the seal. Within was another sealed envelope. Its cover read, "Not to be opened until the death or disappearance of Dr. Henry Jekyll." Utterson was alarmed. As in Jekyll's will, here was the idea of Jekyll's disappearing. Months ago, Utterson had returned the will to Jekyll, at Jekyll's request. The will's reference to Jekyll's possible disappearance had, Utterson believed, been Hyde's sinister idea. Hyde must have intended to murder Jekyll. But why would Lanyon suggest that Jekyll might disappear? Utterson was greatly tempted to disregard the prohibition, open the envelope, and immediately learn the answer. However, professional honor and loyalty to his dead friend were strong obligations. The envelope remained in his safe.

From that day, Utterson felt less desire for Jekyll's company. He thought kindly of Jekyll, but his thoughts were troubled and fearful. He periodically called on Jekyll, but he was relieved to be denied entry. In his heart, he preferred to speak to Poole on the doorstep, surrounded by the open air and sounds of the city, rather than enter that house of voluntary bondage and speak with its mysterious recluse. Indeed, Poole had no pleasant news to communicate. Jekyll, it seemed, now confined himself to the laboratory more than ever. Sometimes he even would sleep there. He was out of spirits, had grown silent, and didn't read. He seemed troubled. Utterson became so used to the unvarying character of these reports that his visits gradually became less frequent.

CHAPTER 7

Incident at the Window

Utterson and Enfield see Jekyll sitting at his window. Jekyll looks sad and then terrified.

By chance, when they were on their usual Sunday walk together, Utterson and Enfield once again arrived before the street door to Jekyll's science building. Both stopped to look at it.

"Well, that story finally has ended," Enfield said. "We won't ever see Hyde again."

"I hope not," Utterson said. "Did I ever tell you that I saw him once and shared your feeling of revulsion?"

"It was impossible to see him *without* feeling revulsion," Enfield said. "By the way, you must have thought me a fool because I didn't know that this door is a rear entrance to Jekyll's residence."

"Not at all," Utterson said.

"I learned that some time later," Enfield added.

After a pause, Utterson said, "Let's step into the courtyard and take a look at the windows. To tell you the truth, I'm worried about Henry Jekyll. The presence of a friend, even one standing outside, might do him some good."

The courtyard was cool, somewhat damp, and darkening with twilight, even though the sky overhead still was bright with the setting sun. The middle one of the three windows was half open. Utterson saw Jekyll sitting beside it, like some despairing prisoner, taking the air with an expression of infinite sadness.

"Henry!" Utterson cried. "Are you feeling better?"

"I'm very low, Gabriel," Jekyll replied drearily. "Thank God, it won't last long."

"You stay indoors too much," Utterson said. "You should be outside, whipping up the circulation—like Enfield and me. This is my cousin, Mr. Richard Enfield. Richard, Dr. Henry Jekyll. Get your hat and come walk with us."

"That's good of you," Jekyll sighed. "I'd like to, very much, but it's impossible. No, I don't dare. But indeed, Gabriel, I'm very glad to see you. It's a great pleasure. I'd ask you and your cousin to come in, but the place really isn't fit."

"Well, then," Utterson said good-naturedly, "the best thing we can do is stay down here and speak with you from here."

"That is just what I was about to suggest," Jekyll said with a smile. But he hardly had uttered the words when the smile was replaced by an expression of such terror and despair that it froze the blood of the two gentlemen below. They merely glimpsed it, because the window instantly was closed. But that glimpse sufficed.

Utterson and Enfield turned and left the courtyard in silence. In silence, too, they walked down the street.

It wasn't until they had come to a neighboring thoroughfare, where even on a Sunday there were stirrings of life, that Utterson turned and looked at Enfield. They both were pale. Each had horror in his eyes.

"God help us all," Utterson said.

Enfield nodded gravely, and they walked on in silence.

CHAPTER 8

The Last Night

Fearing that Hyde has murdered Jekyll, Jekyll's butler Poole comes to Utterson for help. Poole and Utterson break down the door to Jekyll's laboratory, but they find Hyde, not Jekyll, lying dead.

One evening after dinner, Utterson was sitting by his fireside when he was surprised by a visit from Poole.

"Bless me, Poole, what brings you here?" Utterson asked. "Is Dr. Jekyll ill?"

"Mr. Utterson, something is wrong."

"Take a seat. Here's a glass of wine for you. Take your time, and tell me plainly what this is about."

"You know the doctor's ways, sir, and how he shuts himself up," Poole said. "Well, he's shut up again in the laboratory, and I don't like it, sir. I feel afraid."

"My good man, be specific," Utterson said. "What are you afraid of?"

"I've been afraid for about a week," Poole said, "and I can't bear it anymore."

Poole's appearance attested to his words. His manner had changed for the worse. Except for the moment when he had first announced his terror, he hadn't looked Utterson in the face a single time. Even now, he sat with the glass of wine, untasted, on his knee and his eyes directed to a corner of the floor. "I can't bear it anymore," he repeated.

"I see that you have some good reason, Poole. I see that something is seriously wrong. Try to tell me what it is."

"I think there's been foul play," Poole said hoarsely.

"Foul play!" Utterson cried. "What foul play?"

"I dare not say, sir. Please come with me and see for yourself."

Utterson rose and got his hat and coat. He observed the great relief that appeared on Poole's face.

Poole placed the glass of wine, still untasted, on a table and followed Utterson.

It was a wild, cold March night, with a pale crescent moon lying on its back as if tilted by the wind. Debris blew about. The wind made talking difficult and reddened the face. It seemed to have swept the streets bare of pedestrians.

Utterson thought he never had seen that part of London so deserted. He wished otherwise. Never in his life had he felt such a strong desire for the presence of others. As much as he struggled against the feeling, he had a powerful sense of coming disaster.

When Utterson and Poole reached Jekyll's front yard, it was full of wind and dust. Thin trees lashed the railing.

Poole, who had continually kept a pace or two ahead, stopped in the middle of the pavement leading up to the house. Despite the biting weather, he removed his hat and mopped his brow with a handkerchief. Although he had hurried, he wasn't wiping away the sweat of exertion but the sweat of fear. His face was white.

At the door to Jekyll's residence, Poole said in a hoarse, broken voice, "Well, sir, here we are. God grant that nothing is wrong."

"Amen," Utterson said.

Poole knocked in a very guarded way. The door was opened on the chain, and a servant asked, "Is that you, Poole?"

"It's all right," Poole said. "Open the door."

When Poole and Utterson entered, the hall was brightly lit and the fire high. Huddled together like a flock of sheep, all of Jekyll's servants stood around the hearth.

At the sight of Utterson, the housemaid broke into hysterical whimpering.

The cook cried, "Thank God, it's Mr. Utterson!" and ran forward as if to take him in her arms.

"Why are all of you here?" Utterson asked.

"They're all afraid," Poole said.

Blank silence followed. Then the maid wept loudly. All the other servants started and turned toward the inner door with faces of dread.

"Silence!" Poole commanded with a ferocity that testified to his jangled nerves. "Bring me a candle," he said to the kitchen boy. When the boy had brought the candle, Poole said, "Mr. Utterson, please follow me," and led the way to the backyard. "Come as quietly as you can, sir. I want you to hear without being heard. If by any chance he asks you to come inside the laboratory, don't go."

Utterson's nerves were so jolted that he nearly lost his balance. He followed Poole through the surgery theater to the foot of the stairs leading up to Jekyll's laboratory. Here Poole motioned to Utterson that he should stand to one side and listen.

Gathering his courage, Poole set the candle down, mounted the stairs, and knocked on the laboratory door with a shaking hand. "Mr.

Utterson is here to see you, sir," he called, signaling to Utterson that he should listen.

From within, a voice answered, "Tell him I can't see anyone."

"Thank you, sir," Poole responded.

Taking up his candle, Poole led Utterson back across the yard and into the kitchen. Looking Utterson in the eyes, Poole said, "Sir, was that my master's voice?"

Returning Poole's look, Utterson answered, "It seemed very different."

"Different? I certainly think so," Poole said. "Have I been in Dr. Jekyll's service twenty years without being able to recognize his voice? No, sir. My master has been murdered. He was murdered eight days ago when we heard him cry out to God. Whoever is in there isn't Dr. Jekyll."

"Suppose what you say is true, and Dr. Jekyll has been . . . murdered. Why would the murderer stay? That doesn't make sense."

"For a week, whoever is in the laboratory has been crying night and day for some sort of medicine. Sometimes Dr. Jekyll would write prescriptions and place them on the stairs leading up to the laboratory. For a week, the door to the laboratory has remained closed. The meals we've left outside it have been taken in when no one was looking. Every day—sometimes two or three times a day—prescriptions have been placed on the stairs. I've hurried from one pharmacy to another. Each time that I brought back medicine, a note soon told me to return it because it wasn't pure, and there was another prescription. Whoever is in that laboratory is desperate for this drug."

"Do you have any of the notes or prescriptions?" Utterson asked.

Poole reached into his pocket and took out a crumpled note.

Bending closer to the candle, Utterson silently read a note from Jekyll addressed to a well-known pharmacy: "The last sample was impure and useless for my present purposes. Having previously purchased a large quantity from you, I beg you to search with great care for more of adequate purity. If you find any, please forward it to me immediately. Expense is no consideration. I can't exaggerate the importance of this."

"This is a strange note," Utterson said. "Why has it been opened?"

"The pharmacist was very angry, sir. He threw it back at me after he opened it."

"You're sure that Dr. Jekyll wrote this?"

"I thought it looked like his handwriting, but . . ." Poole hesitated. "Today I came suddenly into the surgery theater from the backyard. At first, because the laboratory door was open, I thought that Dr. Jekyll must have slipped out to look for this drug. Someone was at the far end of the surgery theater, digging among the crates. When I came in, he looked up, cried out, and hurried upstairs into the laboratory. I saw him for only a minute, but the hair stood up on my head like quills. If that was my master, why was his face so different? Why did he cry out and run from me?" Poole passed his hand over his face.

"I think I begin to understand," Utterson said. "Your master must be seized with an illness that tortures and deforms the sufferer. That would explain the change in his voice and face and his avoidance of his friends. That would explain why he's desperate to find this drug, which might offer some hope of recovery. All of this is sad but no cause for terror."

"Sir," Poole said respectfully but firmly, "the creature I saw wasn't my master." He looked around to make sure that no one was within hearing and said softly, "My master is a tall, well-built man. This was more of a dwarf. Do you think I don't know my master after twenty years? Do you think I don't know how tall he stands in the laboratory doorway, where I saw him every morning? No, sir, that thing wasn't Dr. Jekyll. God knows what it was, but it wasn't Dr. Jekyll. I believe with all my heart that Dr. Jekyll has been murdered."

"In that case, Poole, I have to break down the door."

"Yes, let's do that, sir!" Poole cried. "There's an ax in the surgery theater, and you can take the kitchen poker for yourself."

Utterson took up the heavy poker. "You know—don't you, Poole?—that we're about to place ourselves in grave danger."

"Indeed I do, sir," Poole replied.

"This creature that you saw . . . Was it . . .? Was it Mr. Hyde?"

"Well, sir, it went so quick and was so doubled up that I couldn't swear to it, but—yes—I think it was. It was his size and had the same quick, light way. And who else could have got in by the laboratory door? At the time of the murder, he still had a key. Did you ever meet Mr. Hyde, sir?"

"Yes. I spoke with him once."

"Then, you must know as well as the rest of us that there's something strange about him, something unsettling. I don't know how to say it, sir, beyond this: he makes a person's blood turn cold and thin."

"Yes," Utterson said.

"When that monkey-like thing jumped from among the chemicals and whipped into the laboratory, an icy feeling shot down my spine. I'm certain it was Mr. Hyde!"

"Yes, I fear so. Evil was sure to come from Dr. Jekyll's association with him. I believe, as you do, that Hyde has murdered Dr. Jekyll. I believe that Hyde—for what purpose, God alone knows—is still in the laboratory. Call Bradshaw."

The footman, white and nervous, came at the summons.

"Pull yourself together, Bradshaw," Utterson said. "This suspense, I know, has taken a toll on all of you. It's about to end. Poole and I are going to force our way into the laboratory. I accept full responsibility for the property damage. In case someone tries to escape out the back way, you and the kitchen boy must go around the corner with a pair of good sticks and take your post at the laboratory door. We'll give you ten minutes to get to your stations."

As Bradshaw left, Utterson looked at his watch. "Now, Poole, let's get to ours."

Taking the poker under his arm, Utterson led the way into the courtyard. Clouds now covered the moon, so it was dark. The wind tossed the light of the candle to and fro until Utterson and Poole entered the surgery theater, where they sat down silently to wait. The stillness was broken only by the footsteps of someone moving back and forth across the laboratory floor.

"He walks like that all day, sir," Poole whispered, "and most of the night. There's a bit of a break only when a new drug sample comes from the pharmacist. It's a guilty conscience that causes such restlessness. Blood has been foully shed. Listen, sir. Listen carefully. Those footsteps aren't the doctor's."

The steps fell lightly and slowly, with an odd swing. They were very different from Jekyll's heavy, creaking tread.

"Sometimes he weeps," Poole said.

"Weeps?" Utterson was chilled with horror.

"Weeps like a woman or a lost soul," Poole continued.

The ten minutes drew to an end. Poole took the ax out from under a stack of packing straw. He set the candle on the nearest table and, scarcely breathing, drew near to where the footsteps continued up and down, up and down.

"Jekyll, I demand to see you!" Utterson said loudly.

No reply.

"Open the door, or we'll break it down!" Utterson shouted.

"Utterson," a voice from within answered, "for God's sake, have mercy!"

"That isn't Dr. Jekyll's voice. It's Hyde's!" Utterson cried. "Down with the door, Poole!"

Poole swung the ax over his shoulder. The blow shook the building, and the door leaped against its hinges.

A screech, as of an animal in terror, rang from the laboratory.

The ax swung again. The door panels crashed, and the frame bounded. Four times the blow fell, but the wood was tough and the fittings well-made. It wasn't until the fifth blow that the lock burst and the wreck of the door fell inwards onto the carpet.

Utterson and Poole, appalled by their own violence and the stillness that followed, stood back a little and peered in. The laboratory was bathed in quiet lamplight. A good fire glowed and crackled on the hearth. A tea kettle sang a thin strain. Utterson and Poole saw two open drawers, papers neatly set out on Jekyll's desk, and, nearer the fire, a teacup and spoon on a saucer. Except for the glassware full of chemicals, you would have thought the room the quietest and most commonplace in London.

In the middle of the room, a man's body lay face down, still contorted and twitching. Utterson and Poole drew near, turned the body over, and beheld the face of Edward Hyde. He was dressed in clothes far too large for him, clothes of Jekyll's size. The muscles of his face still moved with the appearance of life, but he was dead. From the strong chemical smell and the crushed vial in Hyde's hand, Utterson knew that Hyde had committed suicide.

"We've come too late to either save or punish," Utterson said. "Hyde is dead. The only thing left to do is to find your master's body."

Utterson and Poole searched the entire science building, including its few dark closets and spacious cellar. Every closet was empty. Dust fell from the closet doors, indicating that they hadn't been opened in a long time. A mat of cobwebs had long sealed the cellar door. This mat fell as Utterson and Poole opened the door. There was no trace of Jekyll, dead or alive.

Poole stomped on the hallway's floorboards. "Dr. Jekyll must be buried under these."

"Maybe he fled," Utterson said with some hope. He turned to examine the door on the side street. It was locked. He found the key, rusting, lying nearby. "The key doesn't look used," Utterson said.

"It's broken," Poole said, "as if someone stomped on it."

"Yes," Utterson said, "and the cracks are rusty."

The two men looked at each other.

"This is beyond me, Poole," Utterson said. "Let's go back to the laboratory."

They climbed the stairs in silence.

With an occasional awestruck glance at Hyde's corpse, Utterson and Poole examined the laboratory's contents. At one table there were traces of chemical work. In heaps of varying amounts, a white salt lay on glass saucers, as if for an experiment.

"This is the drug that I always was bringing him," Poole said.

As Poole spoke, the kettle boiled over with a startling noise. This brought Utterson and Poole to the fireside. An easy chair sat cozily nearby, with tea things beside it. The cup had sugar in it. There were several books on a shelf. Another book lay open beside the tea things. Utterson was amazed to see that it was a religious work for which Jekyll had expressed great esteem. Startling blasphemies were written in it, in Jekyll's hand.

Utterson and Poole next came to the tall, free-standing mirror. It was tilted so that it showed the fire's rosy glow playing on the ceiling, the fire sparkling in a hundred places on the laboratory's glassware, and their own pale, fearful faces.

"That mirror has seen some strange things, sir," Poole said softly.

"The mirror itself is strange," Utterson said. "What on earth could Dr. Jekyll want with it?"

Next they turned to Jekyll's desk. A large envelope lay on top of neatly arranged papers. It was addressed, in Jekyll's handwriting, to Utterson. Utterson opened it, and several enclosures fell to the floor. The first was a will, drawn in the same eccentric terms as the one that Utterson had returned to Jekyll six months before. It, too, mentioned Jekyll's possible disappearance. However, in place of the name of Edward Hyde, Utterson read, with amazement, his own name. He looked at Poole, then back at the will, and finally at the dead evildoer stretched on the carpet.

"My head spins," Utterson said. "Hyde has been here. Why didn't he read and destroy this document, which displaces him as Jekyll's heir?"

Utterson picked up another paper. It was a brief note in Jekyll's hand and dated at the top. "Poole!" Utterson cried. "Dr. Jekyll was here today. He can't have been killed and hidden in such a short time. He must still be alive! He must have fled!"

Utterson brought the note to his eyes and silently read:

My dear Gabriel,

When this falls into your hands, I will have disappeared. I can't foresee the circumstances, but my instinct and situation tell me that the end is certain and near. Read the narrative that Lanyon told me he was going to place in your hands. If, after that, you want to know more, turn to the confession of

Your unworthy and unhappy friend,
Henry Jekyll

"Wasn't there a third enclosure?" Utterson asked.

"Here, sir," Poole said, handing Utterson a large packet sealed in several places.

Utterson put it into his pocket. "Don't say anything about this note, Poole. If your master has fled or is dead, we can at least save his reputation. It's ten o'clock. I must go home and read these documents in solitude. But I'll be back before midnight, when we'll send for the police."

They went out, locking the door to the surgery theater behind them. Utterson, once again leaving the servants gathered around the hall fireplace, trudged back to his office to read the two narratives that would explain this mystery.

CHAPTER 9

Dr. Lanyon's Narrative

*In a letter to Utterson, Lanyon describes how
Hyde came to Lanyon's house and, by drinking a
potion, transformed himself into Jekyll.*

Four days ago, on January 9, the mail carrier delivered a registered envelope from my colleague and old school companion Dr. Henry Jekyll. This greatly surprised me because we weren't in the habit of corresponding. I had dined with Jekyll the previous evening, and I couldn't imagine anything that would call for such formality between us. The contents increased my wonder. The letter read as follows:

December 10, 1886

Dear Hastie,

You're one of my oldest friends. Although we sometimes have differed on scientific questions, I can't remember any break in our affection—at least, not on my side. There never was a day when, if you had said to me, "Henry, my life, honor, and sanity depend on you," I wouldn't have sacrificed my left hand to help you. Hastie, my life, honor, and sanity now depend on *you*. If you fail me tonight, I'm lost.

Please postpone all other engagements for tonight and, with this letter in your hand for instructions, come straight to my house. Poole has received his instructions. You'll find him waiting for you with a locksmith. Force open the door of my laboratory, and enter alone. Open the tallest cabinet. If it's locked, break the lock. Remove the fourth drawer from the top with all its contents, including some powders, a vial, and a logbook. Take this drawer back to your house.

At midnight, when all your servants are in bed, be alone in your consulting room. Admit into your house a man who will present himself in my name. Give him the drawer that you will have taken from my laboratory, and thereby earn my complete gratitude.

These arrangements are of the utmost importance. Neglecting any of them, strange as they must seem, might result in

my insanity or death. I beg you to heed this
appeal. Save

Your friend,
Henry Jekyll

P.S. I had already sealed this letter when a
fresh terror struck me. The post office
might fail me and not deliver this letter
until tomorrow morning. In that case, do
what I ask when it is most convenient for
you during the day and once again expect
my messenger at midnight. It may then
already be too late. If no messenger comes,
you'll know that you've seen the last of me.

Upon reading this letter, I believed that
Jekyll was insane. However, until that was
proven, I felt bound to do as he asked. Such an
intense, urgent appeal couldn't be dismissed
without possibly grave consequences. So I rose
from the table, got into a carriage, and headed
straight to Jekyll's house.

Poole was awaiting my arrival. He had
received a registered letter of instructions and
had sent at once for a locksmith.

The locksmith came while Poole and I were
talking. The three of us headed to the surgery
theater. The door to Jekyll's laboratory was very
strong and the lock excellent. It took the locksmith nearly two hours to open the lock.

I found the tallest cabinet unlocked. I removed the fourth drawer, had it filled with straw and tied in a sheet, and returned home with it.

I examined its contents. The powders were plainly of Jekyll's own making. When I opened one of the wrappers, I found what seemed to be a simple white salt. Next I turned my attention to the vial. It was about half filled with a blood-red liquid that had a highly pungent odor and seemed to contain phosphorus and ether. I had no idea what the other ingredients were.

The logbook had little written in it other than a series of dates. These spanned many years. but the entries abruptly ceased nearly a year ago. Here and there a brief remark, usually no more than a single word, accompanied a date. "Double" appeared about six times in a total of several hundred entries. "Total failure!" appeared once, early in the list.

Although all of this aroused my curiosity, it told me little. The drawer contained a vial of some kind of salt and the record of a series of experiments that had produced (like too many of Jekyll's investigations) no useful results. How could the presence of these items in my house affect the honor, sanity, or life of my eccentric colleague? Why was a messenger coming to me, and in secret? The more I reflected, the more instead, I explain the situation, you'll have new knowledge and new avenues to fame and power, but your current beliefs will be shattered."

Pretending to be calm, I said, "Sir, you speak in riddles, and I doubt the truth of your words. But I desire an explanation of this strange situation."

"Very well," my visitor replied. "You, Lanyon, have had narrow views of reality. You've denied everything that science, as you know it, couldn't explain. You've mocked your betters. Now—behold!"

He put the glass to his lips and drank the mixture in one gulp. A cry followed. He reeled, staggered, clutched at the table, and held on. Staring and gasping, he swelled. His face turned black, and his features melted.

I sprang to my feet and leaped back against the wall. My arms were raised to shield me from what I saw. I was overcome with terror. "Oh, God!" I screamed again and again.

There before my eyes—pale, shaken, groping, half fainting, like a man restored from death—there stood Henry Jekyll!

Now that the sight of the miraculous transformation has faded from my eyes, I ask myself if it really happened. I'm completely at a loss to explain it. My life is shaken to its roots. I can't sleep anymore. All hours of the day and night, I

convinced I became that Jekyll was mentally ill. I dismissed my servants to bed but loaded an old revolver, so that I would have some means of self-defense.

Midnight had scarcely rung out over London when the door-knocker gently sounded. I went to the door and found a small man crouching against the porch's pillars. "Have you come from Dr. Jekyll?" I asked.

"Yes," he said. When I asked him to enter, he first glanced backward into the darkness of the square. There was a policeman not far off, advancing with an open lantern. My visitor started at the sight and hurried inside.

These particulars struck me disagreeably. As I followed the visitor into the bright light of my consulting room, I kept my hand on my revolver. Now I saw him clearly. I never had seen him before. In addition to his smallness, I was struck by his face—a remarkable combination of great muscular activity and apparent sickliness. His presence greatly disturbed me. I assumed that I simply felt some personal distaste, but the sharpness of that distaste puzzled me. Since then, I've concluded that my revulsion was an instinctive response to evil.

This person, who aroused such disgust in me, was dressed in a way that would have made an ordinary person laughable. Although his clothes were of rich and tasteful fabric, they were enormously too large for him in every measurement. His trousers were rolled up to keep them from dragging along the ground. The waist of his jacket fell below his hips. His collar sprawled on his shoulders. Far from feeling inclined to laugh, I felt sharp repugnance and a keen curiosity about his origin, character, life, fortune, and status.

My visitor was greatly excited. "Do you have it?" he cried. "Do you have it?" He was so impatient that he laid his hand on my arm and started to shake me.

His touch made my blood icy. I pulled away. "Come, sir," I said. "I haven't even made your acquaintance. Please be seated." I sat down in my customary seat, making every effort to appear at ease in spite of my horror.

"Quite right, Dr. Lanyon," he said. "I beg your pardon. My impatience has overcome politeness. I am here at the bidding of your colleague, Dr. Henry Jekyll, on important business." He paused and put his hand to his throat. In spite of his collected manner, he was wrestling against hysteria. "I've been told that a drawer . . ."

Taking pity on him, I said, "There it is, sir." I pointed to the drawer where it lay, still covered with a sheet, on the floor behind a table.

He sprang to it, paused, and laid his on his heart. I could hear his teeth grind his jaw's convulsive action. His face w ghastly that I was alarmed.

"Calm yourself," I said.

He gave me a dreadful smile and pulle sheet away. At the sight of the content uttered a loud sob of immense relief. The moment, in a voice fairly well under contro asked, "Do you have a measuring glass?"

With some effort, I rose and gave hi measuring glass.

He thanked me with a smiling nod, m ured out a very small amount of the red liq and added one of the powders. The mixt which was reddish at first, brightened in colo the crystals melted. It audibly bubbled and g off small fumes. Suddenly the bubbling cease and the compound changed to dark pur which faded to watery green.

My visitor, who had keenly watched th changes, smiled, set the glass down on the tab and turned and looked at me with an air examination. "Now," he said, "will you be w and allow me to take this glass in my hand a leave your house without further talk? Or you too curious for that? Think before y answer because I'll do as you choose. If I rem silent, you'll be neither richer nor wiser.

feel terror. I know that I'm dying.

I can't bring myself to write down what Jekyll told me during the hour that followed the transformation. It sickened my soul. With tears of repentance, Jekyll confessed to deeds too horrible for me to relate. I'll say one thing, Gabriel: by Jekyll's own admission, the creature who entered my house that night was known by the name of Edward Hyde and was hunted throughout England as Sir Danvers's murderer.

CHAPTER 10

Henry Jekyll's Full Statement of the Case

In a written confession, Jekyll explains how he developed a potion that turned him into a monster.

I was born into a wealthy family in 1835. As a child and young man, I was physically fit, hard-working, eager to be respected by wise and good people, and thus headed toward an honorable and distinguished future. My worst fault was a love of merriment that was hard to reconcile with my desire to appear to be of the highest seriousness. I ended up concealing my pleasures.

When I reached maturity and took stock of my progress and position in the world, I found that I was committed to a profound duplicity. Many people would have felt no shame at inconsistencies in their character and behavior, and no need to conceal them. But I had set myself such high standards that I hid these inconsistencies with an almost morbid sense of shame. Good and evil were more sharply divided, and more at odds, in me than in most people. Both sides of me were in dead earnest. I was myself when I gave in, unrestrained, to temptation. I also was myself when I worked to advance knowledge or relieve suffering.

My scientific studies shed light on the continual war within me. With every passing day, I became more convinced that, both morally and intellectually, a person isn't really one being, but two. Like other people, I had two competing natures. I told myself, "If each of these natures could be housed in a separate identity, people would be relieved of all that is unbearable. Unjust people would be spared the feelings of guilt that righteous people suffer, and righteous people would walk steadfastly and securely on their upward path, doing the good things in which they find pleasure and no longer tormented by temptations." It was the curse of humankind that these conflicting elements were bound together.

Laboratory experiments began to give me hope that I could separate these elements. I mixed a drug that I thought might separate out everything base within an individual. I hesitated a long time before I tested my theory. After all,

I was risking death, especially if I took too high a dose. But the possibility of so great a discovery overcame my fears. Having long ago prepared the rest of the drug, I purchased a large quantity of a particular salt that I knew, from my experiments, was the last required ingredient. Late one night, I mixed the ingredients and watched them boil and smoke in the glass. When the bubbling subsided, I, with a strong glow of courage, drank the potion.

Racking suffering followed: nausea, a grinding in my bones, horror. But these agonies swiftly subsided. They were replaced by new, sweet sensations. I felt younger, lighter, happier. I felt a liberating recklessness. Disordered sensual images ran through my mind. The bonds of obligation dissolved. I felt an unknown, but not innocent, freedom. I immediately knew that I was more wicked—ten times more wicked— than before. I felt abandoned to evil. Like wine, the thought braced and delighted me. I stretched out my hands, exulting in the freshness of my sensations.

Suddenly I was aware that I was much shorter than before. At the time, there was no mirror in my laboratory. The one that now stands beside me was brought there later so that I could witness my transformations. It was shortly before dawn. All of my servants were asleep. Flushed with hope and triumph, I ventured, in my new shape, to my bedroom. I crossed the courtyard and crept through the hallways, a stranger in my own house. Upon reaching my room, I saw for the first time the appearance of Edward Hyde.

I concluded that my nature's evil side, to which I now had given form, was weaker and less developed than its good side, which I had discarded. After all, nine-tenths of my life had been exemplary in effort, virtue, and control. For this reason, I think, Edward Hyde was much smaller, weaker, and younger than Henry Jekyll. Just as goodness shone in Jekyll's face, evil was plainly written on Hyde's. Evil also had left an imprint of deformity and decay on Hyde's body. Yet, when I looked at that ugly being in the mirror, I felt no repugnance, but a leap of welcome. This, too, was myself. It seemed natural and human. In my eyes it was livelier and more interesting than the imperfect, divided individual I previously had been. Later I would observe that every person who encountered Hyde reacted with revulsion. This, I believe, is because all human beings are a mixture of good and evil. Only Hyde was pure evil.

For only a moment, I lingered at the mirror. I didn't know if I had lost my former identity forever and must flee, before daylight, from a house that no longer was mine.

Hurrying back to my laboratory, I once again prepared and drank the potion and suffered the pangs of transformation. I returned to the character, stature, and face of Henry Jekyll.

I now had the ability to be two separate individuals. One was wholly evil. The other, the old Henry Jekyll, was a mixture of good and evil. I never had fully conquered my dislike of an entirely dry life of study. I still wanted, at times, to indulge in unworthy pleasures. However, I was well-known and highly respected. I also was middle-aged. So it was increasingly awkward, if not impossible, for me to indulge my desires as Henry Jekyll. Now all I had to do was drink the potion and I could become someone else, someone free to do as he pleased: Edward Hyde. I smiled at the notion. At the time, my plan struck me as amusing.

In preparation, I bought and furnished the Soho house to which the police tracked Hyde. I hired a housekeeper I knew to be silent and unscrupulous. I announced to my servants that a Mr. Hyde (whom I described) was to have full liberty and power around my house. Next I drew up the will to which you so strongly objected, so that if anything happened to me, Henry Jekyll, I could continue to be Edward Hyde and keep all of my possessions.

People sometimes hire others to commit crimes in their behalf while they themselves remain safe and respected. In a way, I was doing that, for the sake of pleasure. The public would continue to regard Henry Jekyll as kind and respectable, yet I would be able to plunge into a sea of liberty. Cloaked with a completely different identity, I would be completely safe. Let me but escape into my laboratory, give me a second or two to mix and swallow the potion that I always had standing ready, and, whatever he had done, Hyde would evaporate like breath on a mirror. In his place, quietly at home, studying by the lamplight, would be Henry Jekyll.

In my disguise, I made haste to indulge in undignified pleasures. In Hyde's hands, these pleasures soon turned monstrous. When I would return from my adventures as Hyde, I often was plunged into a kind of wonder at the depravity I enjoyed through him. Hyde was entirely villainous. All of his actions and thoughts were self-centered. He took pleasure in others' suffering. Initially, I was horrified by Hyde's actions. But the situation caused my conscience to deteriorate. I told myself that it was Hyde—not Jekyll—who was guilty. I was the same good fellow as before. I even would make haste, whenever possible, to undo the evil done by Hyde. So my conscience slept.

I won't detail the evils that I committed. (Even now, I scarcely can admit that I committed them.) I'll mention only those events that led to my complete downfall. For example, I committed an act of cruelty to a child that aroused the anger of a passerby. The other day, I recognized this same man as your cousin Richard Enfield. A doctor and the child's family also felt fury toward Hyde, so there were moments when I feared for my life. At last, to calm their justified anger, Hyde brought them to my house and gave the family a check bearing my signature. As a result of this incident, I opened an account in Hyde's name at another bank. To give Hyde a signature different from my own, I wrote with my hand slanted backward. My plotting made me think that I was safe.

About two months before Sir Danvers's murder, I returned home at a late hour after one of my adventures as Hyde. The next day I awoke feeling strange. I looked around and saw my bedroom's fine furniture and tall walls. I also saw the familiar pattern of my bed curtains and the familiar design of my bed's mahogany frame. Why, then, did I have the uncomfortable feeling that, instead of being in my own bed, I was in the small room in Soho where I was accustomed to sleep as Hyde? Dismissing the feeling, I dropped back into a comfortable morning doze.

When I next awoke, my eyes fell on my hand. My hands are large, firm, white, and handsome. But the hand that I now saw clearly in the mid-morning light, lying half closed on the bedspread, was thin, wiry, heavy-knuckled, dark, and hairy. It was Hyde's hand.

Stunned, I stared at it for about half a minute. I felt terror as startling as a cymbal crash. Bounding from my bed, I rushed to the mirror. My blood turned thin and icy at the sight that met my eyes. I had gone to bed as Henry Jekyll but awakened as Edward Hyde. How could this be? What could I do? I stood horror-struck.

The servants were up and about. All of my drugs were in the laboratory—a journey down two flights of stairs, through the back passage, across the open courtyard, and through the surgery theater. I could conceal my face, but that wouldn't hide the dramatic change in my height. With tremendous relief, I remembered that the servants already were accustomed to seeing Hyde come and go.

I quickly dressed in my own clothes, which were much too large for Hyde, and passed through the house. Bradshaw stared and drew back at seeing Hyde in the morning and so strangely dressed.

Ten minutes later, I had returned to my own shape and was sitting down to breakfast.

But I had little appetite. This inexplicable incident—a reversal of my previous experience—seemed to signal my doom. I thought more seriously than ever before about the possible consequences of my double existence. Lately I had provided the evil part of myself with much exercise and nourishment. Hyde's body had grown somewhat taller and stronger. I began to recognize a danger that, if I continued changing into Hyde, the balance of my character might permanently shift to the evil side, and I might lose the power to change back into Jekyll, with Hyde's character becoming irreversibly mine.

The drug's power to turn me back into Jekyll hadn't always been consistent. Once, early in my experiment, it had totally failed me. Since then I sometimes had needed to double the dose. Once, at a high risk of death, I even had tripled the dose.

In the beginning it had been difficult to change from Jekyll to Hyde. Lately it was more difficult to change from Hyde to Jekyll. Slowly but surely I was losing hold of my original and better self. More and more, my worse nature was taking over.

I now felt I had to choose between good and evil, Jekyll and Hyde. Jekyll shared in Hyde's pleasures and adventures—sometimes with fear, sometimes with greedy eagerness.

Hyde, in contrast, was indifferent to Jekyll except to regard him the way a robber regards his hideout. If I chose to be Jekyll, I no longer could indulge the appetites that I had come to pamper. If I chose to be Hyde, I had to say goodbye to many interests and aspirations and become, forever, friendless and despised. But there was another important consideration: whereas Jekyll would suffer sharply at no longer being able to indulge himself, Hyde wouldn't be aware of having lost anything. That happy ignorance was sorely tempting. Nevertheless, I chose Jekyll. I preferred the aging, discontented doctor, surrounded by friends and cherishing honest hopes. Mustering all my resolve, I said farewell to the liberty, comparative youth, light step, leaping impulses, and secret pleasures that I had enjoyed while disguised as Hyde.

Perhaps I made my choice with some unconscious reluctance, because I kept the Soho house and Hyde's clothes, which remained in my laboratory. For two months I was true to my decision. I led a more self-disciplined life than ever before and enjoyed making amends for my guilty deeds.

Time, however, began to erase the alarm that I had felt. My satisfaction lessened. I began to be tortured by temptation. I longed for Hyde's freedom. Just as an alcoholic hates the loss of awareness and self-control brought on by drunkenness but can't stop drinking, I hated Hyde's readiness to commit evil but desired to be Hyde again.

Finally, in an hour of moral weakness, I again mixed and swallowed the transforming potion. Long caged, the devil in me came out roaring. As soon as I drank the potion, I was aware of a fiercer inclination to evil than ever before.

When Sir Danvers politely asked me for directions, I became enraged for no reason. Filled with glee, I mauled his unresisting body. I delighted in every blow. It was only when I had tired from the physical exertion of beating him to death that I felt terror. Fearing for my life, I fled. Even as I fled, I rejoiced in having killed him. I felt stimulated, intensely alive. I ran to the Soho house and, as a precaution, burned my papers. Then, still gloating about my crime and already planning others, I set out through the lamp-lit streets.

I sang as I prepared the potion. However, as soon as I returned to being Jekyll, I wept with remorse. I fell to my knees and lifted my clasped hands to God. I looked back over my entire life, from my childhood days, when I had walked holding my father's hand, to the self-denying labors of my professional life. With disbelief, I considered the horrific murder that Hyde had committed. Weeping and praying, I recalled hideous sounds and images. As the intensity of my remorse lessened, I felt joy. The problem of my evil conduct was solved. Hyde would cease to exist. With complete sincerity, I vowed that I was done with him. I locked the back door to my science building—the door by which I often had come and gone as Hyde—and ground the key under my heel.

The next day, I learned that someone had witnessed the murder and that the victim was Sir Danvers, a greatly esteemed man. Fear of being arrested and hanged strengthened my resolve never again to become Hyde. Jekyll was my refuge.

I determined to make amends by doing great good. For months I labored to relieve others' suffering. I passed the days quietly, almost happily. Each day, I derived more enjoyment from helping others.

On a fine January day, cloudless overhead but wet underfoot where the frost had melted, I went to the park and sat in the sun on a bench. The park was full of chirping birds and sweet odors. But my evil side soon began to growl. The animal within me licked his mouth, remembering the pleasures he had tasted. I didn't consider becoming Hyde again. The mere thought of that terrified me. However, I smugly thought that I was better than most people because I did so many good deeds.

As soon as I had that conceited, self-satisfied thought, I felt a horrible nausea and deadly shuddering. These passed away and left me faint. Then the faintness subsided, and I became aware of a change in my mood. I felt contemptuous of danger, without obligations. I looked down. My clothes hung formlessly on my shrunken limbs. The hand on my knee was thin and hairy. I was Hyde! A moment before I had been safe, respected, wealthy, and loved, someone who would be served dinner in the comfort of his lovely home. Now I was a fugitive hunted by all, a murderer bound to be hanged.

My drugs were in a drawer of my laboratory. How could I get to them? That was the problem I had to solve. I pressed my hands to my temples. I had left the back door to the science building locked. If I tried to enter by way of the house, my servants would contact the police. I saw that I needed help and thought of Lanyon. How could I make my way to his house without being detected and arrested? How could I, a displeasing stranger, expect him to take something from the laboratory of his colleague, Dr. Jekyll? Then I remembered that I still could write with Jekyll's handwriting.

Arranging my clothes as well as I could, I summoned a passing carriage and was driven to a hotel. The driver couldn't conceal his amusement at my comical appearance. With devilish fury, I gnashed my teeth at him. The smile vanished from his face—luckily for him (and for me) because in another minute I would have attacked him.

As I entered the hotel, I looked around with such an evil expression that the hotel staff trembled. Afraid to look at one another, they took my orders, led me to a private room, and brought me pen and paper. Although enraged and wishing to cause pain, I controlled myself because my life was in danger.

I wrote two important letters, one to Lanyon and one to Poole. To make sure that they would be mailed, I handed them over with instructions that they should be sent by registered mail.

For the rest of the day, I sat in the hotel room, biting my nails. I dined there, alone with my fears. The waiter was visibly afraid of me.

Shortly before midnight, I set out, sitting in the corner of a closed carriage, feeling nothing but fear and hatred. When I arrived at Lanyon's, I saw my old friend's revulsion toward my— Hyde's—appearance and manner.

In front of Lanyon, I took the drug that

restored me to myself. Lanyon, of course, was horrified and expressed strong disapproval of my actions.

I returned to my house and went to bed. I slept deeply but had nightmares.

The next morning, I awoke weak and shaken. I still hated and feared the thought of the brute who slept within me. Nor had I forgotten the previous day's grave dangers. But I was home again, close to my drugs. I felt tremendously grateful for my escape.

After breakfast I strolled across the courtyard. I took pleasure in the chill in the air. Suddenly I felt that I was changing into Hyde. I hurried to my laboratory, where I soon was raging with hatred. It took a double dose of the potion to restore me to Jekyll. Six hours later, as I sat looking sadly into the fire, the pangs returned, and I had to take another dose.

From that day on, I was able to remain Jekyll only by continually taking the drug. At any hour of the day or night, I would feel the shudder that warned me of a coming transformation. Whenever I slept, even if I dozed off only for a moment in my chair, I awoke as Hyde. I tried to get by on so little sleep that I became thin and feverish, weak in body and mind. My sole thought was a horror of being Hyde.

The transformations became so rapid that I

scarcely felt them. As I became more sickly, Hyde became more robust. My two identities now hated each other. I now recognized Hyde as hellish. Hyde needed to hide inside me but resented this need. He also despised my despondency and resented my loathing of him. So he tormented me with apish tricks. In my own handwriting, he wrote blasphemies in my books. He burned my letters and destroyed the portrait of my father. He probably would have killed me if he had been able to do that without bringing about his own end. He feared my power to end his existence by committing suicide.

The situation might have continued for years, but my supply of the salt needed for the potion began to run low. After obtaining a fresh supply, I mixed the potion. The mixture bubbled. The first color change occurred but not the second. I drank the potion, but it was ineffective. I had Poole search London for salt of sufficient purity—in vain. I'm now convinced that the salt I originally used was impure, and whatever made it impure also made it effective.

About a week has passed since I used the last of my original salt supply. Short of a miracle, this is the last time that I'll have the face and thoughts of Henry Jekyll. In fact, I must hurry to conclude this narrative, which has so far escaped destruction only by a combination of

Frankenstein

AFTERWORD

About the Author

Ten days after Mary Wollstonecraft Shelley was born in London in 1797, her mother died of fever. Both of Mary's parents were famous authors. Her mother was Mary Wollstonecraft, author of the groundbreaking feminist book *A Vindication of the Rights of Woman* (1792). Her father was William Godwin, who wrote on politics and philosophy. Other well-known writers often visited Godwin.

At age sixteen, Mary ran off with a married man: poet Percy Bysshe Shelley. Soon after Percy's wife committed suicide in 1816, Mary and Percy married. Of their four children, three died in infancy.

Frankenstein was published in 1818, when Mary was twenty-one. It was a huge success. She wrote other novels, as well as travel books and short stories.

In 1822 Percy drowned while sailing in stormy weather. After a long and productive writing career, Mary died in her sleep in 1851 at the age of fifty-three.

About the Book

Frankenstein shows the disastrous consequences of self-absorption and lack of compassion. The fortunate recipient of much kindness, generosity, and love, Victor Frankenstein rarely treats others with genuine consideration.

Frankenstein becomes so obsessed with his scientific work, especially his experimentation, that he neglects those who love him. For lengthy periods he fails to respond to letters from Elizabeth and his father, even though they're worried by his silence. Also, years pass without his traveling home to see family and friends.

Although his parents lavished him with love, Frankenstein extends no love to *his* "child": the creature he creates. Instead of feeling affection, or even pity, for the creature, Frankenstein feels "horror and disgust," simply because the creature is hideous. Although Frankenstein himself is responsible for the creature's appearance, and although the creature is helpless and entirely innocent, Frankenstein abandons him. As a result, the creature suffers hunger, thirst, cold, and intense loneliness.

When the creature observes the love between a cottager and his two children, the creature feels "deep emotion, a combination of joy and pain." He grieves that no parent ever loved *him*.

Even when the creature tells Frankenstein how much he has suffered, Frankenstein feels almost no pity. Desiring to love and be loved, the creature asks Frankenstein to create a female companion for him. Frankenstein agrees only reluctantly and then breaks his promise.

The creature's rejection by humans, especially Frankenstein, leads to the deaths of William, Henry, Elizabeth, Alphonse, and Frankenstein himself. When Frankenstein has died, the creature weeps. "My heart was shaped to feel love and sympathy," he thinks. "Once, I had hoped to meet with beings who would overlook my appearance and love me for my excellent qualities. No one did. I've always been alone. I've never known any comfort or com-

The Strange Case of
Dr. Jekyll and Mr. Hyde

AFTERWORD

About the Author

Robert Louis Stevenson was born in 1850 in Edinburgh, Scotland. He was the only child of Thomas Stevenson, an engineer, and Margaret Balfour, a minister's daughter.

Robert was a sickly child. To entertain him, his nurse told and read him stories. Before long, Robert began writing stories of his own.

In 1875 Robert received a law degree from the University of Edinburgh. However, instead of practicing law, he became a writer. His first novel, *Treasure Island*, appeared in 1883. The book brought him fame and financial success. His other popular novels include *Kidnapped* (1886) and *The Strange Case of Dr. Jekyll and Mr. Hyde* (1886). Robert also wrote essays, poems, and short stories.

Having married an American divorcée in 1880, Robert traveled around the South Pacific with his wife, stepson, and mother from 1888 to 1890. Then the family settled in Samoa. Robert died of a stroke in 1894 at the age of forty-four.

About the Book

"Both morally and intellectually, a person isn't really one being, but two. Like other people, I had two competing natures," Henry Jekyll writes in *The Strange Case of Dr. Jekyll and Mr. Hyde*. The book dramatizes the conflict, within each of us, between good and evil.

A doctor of medicine and law, Jekyll is a highly respected man: sociable, charitable, hardworking, and religious. His face radiates goodness. Nine-tenths of his life has been "exemplary in effort, virtue, and control." However, he has an evil side, which he indulges whenever he drinks a potion that turns him into Edward Hyde. Completely selfish and cruel, Hyde tramples a little girl and coolly continues on his way. When an elderly gentleman politely asks him for directions, Hyde beats the man to death. He is "pure evil."

The more that Jekyll transforms himself into Hyde, the weaker the good in Jekyll becomes.

As Hyde grows taller and stronger, Jekyll sickens. His conscience deteriorates. It becomes easier for Jekyll to turn into Hyde than vice versa.

Ultimately Jekyll must choose between being Jekyll and being Hyde: between good and evil. He chooses good. But it's too late.

"All human beings are a mixture of good and evil," Jekyll reminds us. His story serves as a warning: if we feed the evil in us, it will grow.

If you liked
Frankenstein and
*The Strange Case of
Dr. Jekyll and Mr. Hyde*
you might be interested in other
books in the Townsend Library.

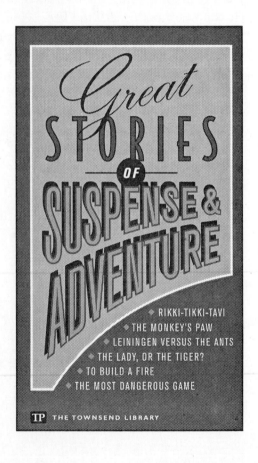

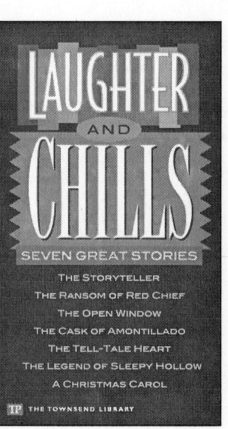

LAUGHTER AND CHILLS

SEVEN GREAT STORIES

THE STORYTELLER

THE RANSOM OF RED CHIEF

THE OPEN WINDOW

THE CASK OF AMONTILLADO

THE TELL-TALE HEART

THE LEGEND OF SLEEPY HOLLOW

A CHRISTMAS CAROL

TP THE TOWNSEND LIBRARY

continued on the following pages

Dracula

BRAM STOKER

THE TOWNSEND LIBRARY TP

The Merry Adventures of

RobinHood

HOWARD PYLE

TP THE TOWNSEND LIBRARY

The Bully

Paul
Langan

convinced I became that Jekyll was mentally ill. I dismissed my servants to bed but loaded an old revolver, so that I would have some means of self-defense.

Midnight had scarcely rung out over London when the door-knocker gently sounded. I went to the door and found a small man crouching against the porch's pillars. "Have you come from Dr. Jekyll?" I asked.

"Yes," he said. When I asked him to enter, he first glanced backward into the darkness of the square. There was a policeman not far off, advancing with an open lantern. My visitor started at the sight and hurried inside.

These particulars struck me disagreeably. As I followed the visitor into the bright light of my consulting room, I kept my hand on my revolver. Now I saw him clearly. I never had seen him before. In addition to his smallness, I was struck by his face—a remarkable combination of great muscular activity and apparent sickliness. His presence greatly disturbed me. I assumed that I simply felt some personal distaste, but the sharpness of that distaste puzzled me. Since then, I've concluded that my revulsion was an instinctive response to evil.

This person, who aroused such disgust in me, was dressed in a way that would have made an ordinary person laughable. Although his clothes were of rich and tasteful fabric, they were enormously too large for him in every measurement. His trousers were rolled up to keep them from dragging along the ground. The waist of his jacket fell below his hips. His collar sprawled on his shoulders. Far from feeling inclined to laugh, I felt sharp repugnance and a keen curiosity about his origin, character, life, fortune, and status.

My visitor was greatly excited. "Do you have it?" he cried. "Do you have it?" He was so impatient that he laid his hand on my arm and started to shake me.

His touch made my blood icy. I pulled away. "Come, sir," I said. "I haven't even made your acquaintance. Please be seated." I sat down in my customary seat, making every effort to appear at ease in spite of my horror.

"Quite right, Dr. Lanyon," he said. "I beg your pardon. My impatience has overcome politeness. I am here at the bidding of your colleague, Dr. Henry Jekyll, on important business." He paused and put his hand to his throat. In spite of his collected manner, he was wrestling against hysteria. "I've been told that a drawer . . ."

Taking pity on him, I said, "There it is, sir." I pointed to the drawer where it lay, still covered with a sheet, on the floor behind a table.

He sprang to it, paused, and laid his hand on his heart. I could hear his teeth grind with his jaw's convulsive action. His face was so ghastly that I was alarmed.

"Calm yourself," I said.

He gave me a dreadful smile and pulled the sheet away. At the sight of the contents, he uttered a loud sob of immense relief. The next moment, in a voice fairly well under control, he asked, "Do you have a measuring glass?"

With some effort, I rose and gave him a measuring glass.

He thanked me with a smiling nod, measured out a very small amount of the red liquid, and added one of the powders. The mixture, which was reddish at first, brightened in color as the crystals melted. It audibly bubbled and gave off small fumes. Suddenly the bubbling ceased, and the compound changed to dark purple, which faded to watery green.

My visitor, who had keenly watched these changes, smiled, set the glass down on the table, and turned and looked at me with an air of examination. "Now," he said, "will you be wise and allow me to take this glass in my hand and leave your house without further talk? Or are you too curious for that? Think before you answer because I'll do as you choose. If I remain silent, you'll be neither richer nor wiser. If, instead, I explain the situation, you'll have new knowledge and new avenues to fame and power, but your current beliefs will be shattered."

Pretending to be calm, I said, "Sir, you speak in riddles, and I doubt the truth of your words. But I desire an explanation of this strange situation."

"Very well," my visitor replied. "You, Lanyon, have had narrow views of reality. You've denied everything that science, as you know it, couldn't explain. You've mocked your betters. Now—behold!"

He put the glass to his lips and drank the mixture in one gulp. A cry followed. He reeled, staggered, clutched at the table, and held on. Staring and gasping, he swelled. His face turned black, and his features melted.

I sprang to my feet and leaped back against the wall. My arms were raised to shield me from what I saw. I was overcome with terror. "Oh, God!" I screamed again and again.

There before my eyes—pale, shaken, groping, half fainting, like a man restored from death—there stood Henry Jekyll!

Now that the sight of the miraculous transformation has faded from my eyes, I ask myself if it really happened. I'm completely at a loss to explain it. My life is shaken to its roots. I can't sleep anymore. All hours of the day and night, I